A HORSE AND TWO GOATS

ALSO BY R.K. NARAYAN

A Horse and Two Goats

STORIES BY

R. K. Narayan

With decorations by R. K. Laxman

THE VIKING PRESS

NEW YORK

First published in 1970 by The Viking Press, Inc.
625 Madison Avenue, New York, N.Y. 10022

SBN 670-37885-2

Library of Congress catalog card number: 70-83229

Printed in U.S.A.

The stories "A Horse and Two Goats," "Seventh House,"
and "Uncle" originally appeared in *The New Yorker,*
in somewhat different form. "A Breath of Lucifer"
originally appeared in *Playboy*.

To my friend Marshall A. Best
to mark a decade (or more) of
the happiest association

Contents

A HORSE AND TWO GOATS

A glossary of the less familiar Indian words will be found on page 147.

A Horse and
Two Goats

Of the seven hundred thousand villages dotting the map of India, in which the majority of India's five hundred million live, flourish, and die, Kritam was probably the tiniest, indicated on the district survey map by a microscopic dot, the map being meant more for the revenue official out to collect tax than for the guidance of the motorist, who in any case could not hope to reach it since it sprawled far from the highway at the end of a rough track furrowed up by the iron-hooped wheels of bullock carts. But its size did not prevent its giving itself the grandiose name Kritam, which meant in Tamil "coronet" or "crown" on the brow of this subcontinent. The village consisted of less than thirty houses, only one of them built with brick and cement. Painted a brilliant yellow and blue all over with gorgeous carvings of gods and gargoyles on its balustrade, it was known as the Big House. The other houses, distributed in four streets, were generally of bamboo thatch, straw, mud, and other unspecified material. Muni's was the last house in the fourth street, beyond which stretched the fields. In his prosperous days Muni had owned a flock of forty sheep and goats and sallied forth every morning driving the flock to the highway a couple of miles away. There he would sit on the pedestal of a clay statue of a horse while his cattle grazed around. He carried a crook at the end of a bamboo pole and snapped foliage from the avenue trees to feed his flock; he also gathered faggots and dry sticks, bundled them, and carried them home for fuel at sunset.

His wife lit the domestic fire at dawn, boiled water in a mud pot, threw into it a handful of millet flour, added salt, and gave him his first nourishment for the day. When he started out, she would put in his hand a packed lunch, once again the same millet cooked into a little ball, which he could swallow with a raw onion at midday. She was old, but he was older and needed all the attention she could give him in order to be kept alive.

His fortunes had declined gradually, unnoticed. From a flock of forty which he drove into a pen at night, his stock had now come down to two goats, which were not worth the rent of a half rupee a month the Big House charged for the use of the pen in their back yard. And so the two goats were tethered to the trunk of a drumstick tree which grew in front of his hut and from which occasionally Muni could shake down drumsticks. This morning he got six. He carried them in with a sense of triumph. Although no one could say precisely who owned the tree, it was his because he lived in its shadow.

She said, "If you were content with the drumstick leaves alone, I could boil and salt some for you."

"Oh, I am tired of eating those leaves. I have a craving to chew the drumstick out of sauce, I tell you."

"You have only four teeth in your jaw, but your craving is for big things. All right, get the stuff for the sauce, and I will prepare it for you. After all, next year you may not be alive to ask for anything. But first get me all the stuff, including a measure of rice or millet, and I will satisfy your unholy craving. Our store is empty today. Dhall, chili, curry leaves, mustard, coriander, gingelley oil, and one large potato. Go out and get all this." He repeated the list after her in order not to miss any item and walked off to the shop in the third street.

He sat on an upturned packing case below the platform of the shop. The shopman paid no attention to him. Muni kept clearing his throat, coughing, and sneezing until the shopman could not stand it any more and demanded, "What ails you? You will fly off that seat into the gutter if you sneeze so hard, young man." Muni laughed inordinately, in order to please the shopman, at being called "young man." The shopman softened and said, "You have enough of the imp inside to keep a second wife busy, but for the fact the old lady is still alive." Muni laughed appropriately again at this joke. It completely won the shopman over; he liked his sense of humour to be appreciated. Muni engaged his attention in local gossip for a few minutes, which always ended with a reference to the postman's wife who had eloped to the city some months before.

The shopman felt most pleased to hear the worst of the postman, who had cheated him. Being an itinerant postman, he returned home to Kritam only once in ten days and every time managed to slip away again without passing the shop in the third street. By thus humouring the shopman, Muni could always ask for one or two items of food, promising repayment later. Some days the shopman was in a good mood and gave in, and sometimes he would lose his temper suddenly and bark at Muni for daring to ask for credit.

This was such a day, and Muni could not progress beyond two items listed as essential components. The shopman was also displaying a remarkable memory for old facts and figures and took out an oblong ledger to support his observations. Muni felt impelled to rise and flee. But his self-respect kept him in his seat and made him listen to the worst things about himself. The shopman concluded, "If you could find five rupees and a quarter, you will have paid off an ancient debt and then could apply for admission to swarga. How much have you got now?"

"I will pay you everything on the first of the next month."

"As always, and whom do you except to rob by then?"

Muni felt caught and mumbled, "My daughter has sent word that she will be sending me money."

"Have you a daughter?" sneered the shopman. "And she is sending you money! For what purpose, may I know?"

"Birthday, fiftieth birthday," said Muni quietly.

"Birthday! How old are you?"

Muni repeated weakly, not being sure of it himself, "Fifty." He always calculated his age from the time of the great famine when he stood as high as the parapet around the village well, but who could calculate such things accurately nowadays with so many famines occurring? The shopman felt encouraged when other customers stood around to watch and comment. Muni thought helplessly, "My poverty is exposed to everybody. But what can I do?"

"More likely you are seventy," said the shopman. "You also forget that you mentioned a birthday five weeks ago when you wanted castor oil for your holy bath."

"Bath! Who can dream of a bath when you have to scratch the tank-bed for a bowl of water? We would all be parched and dead but for the Big House, where they let us take a pot of water from their well." After saying this Muni unobtrusively rose and moved off.

He told his wife, "That scoundrel would not give me anything. So go out and sell the drumsticks for what they are worth."

He flung himself down in a corner to recoup from the fatigue of his visit to the shop. His wife said, "You are getting no sauce today, nor anything else. I can't find anything to give you to eat. Fast till the evening, it'll do you good. Take the goats and be gone now," she cried and added, "Don't come back before the sun is down." He knew that if he obeyed her she would somehow conjure up some food for him in the evening. Only he must be careful not to argue and irritate her. Her temper was undependable in the morning but improved by evening time. She was sure to go out and work—grind corn in the Big House, sweep or scrub somewhere, and earn enough to buy foodstuff and keep a dinner ready for him in the evening.

Unleashing the goats from the drumstick tree, Muni started out, driving them ahead and uttering weird cries from time to time in order to urge them on. He passed through the village with his head bowed in thought. He did not want to look at anyone or be accosted. A couple of cronies lounging in the temple corridor hailed him, but he ignored their call. They had known him in the days of affluence when he lorded over a flock of fleecy sheep, not the miserable gawky goats that he had today. Of course he also used to have a few goats for those who fancied them, but real wealth lay in sheep; they bred fast and people came and bought the fleece in the shearing season; and then that famous butcher from the town came over on the weekly market days bringing him betel leaves, tobacco, and often enough some *bhang,* which they smoked in a hut in the coconut grove, undisturbed by wives and well-wishers. After a smoke one felt light and elated and inclined to forgive everyone including that brother-in-law of his who had once tried to set fire to his home. But all this seemed like the memories of a previous birth. Some pestilence afflicted his cattle (he could of course guess who had laid his animals under a curse), and even the friendly butcher would not touch one at half the price . . . and now here he was left with the two scraggy creatures. He wished someone would rid him of their company too. The shopman had said that he was seventy. At seventy, one only waited to be summoned by God. When he was dead what would his wife do? They had lived in each other's company since they were children. He was told on their day of wedding that he was ten years old and she was eight. During the wedding ceremony they had had to recite their respective ages and names. He had thrashed her only a few times in their career, and later she had the upper hand. Progeny, none. Perhaps a large progeny would have brought him the blessing of the gods. Fertility brought merit. People with fourteen sons were always so prosperous and at peace with the world and themselves. He recollected the thrill he had felt when he mentioned a daughter to that shopman; although it was not believed, what if he did not have a daughter?—his cousin in the next village had many daughters, and any one of them was as good as his; he was fond of them all and would buy them sweets if he could afford it. Still, everyone in the village whispered behind their backs that Muni and his wife were a barren couple. He avoided looking at anyone;

they all professed to be so high up, and everyone else in the village had more money than he. "I am the poorest fellow in our caste and no wonder that they spurn me, but I won't look at them either," and so he passed on with his eyes downcast along the edge of the street, and people left him also very much alone, commenting only to the extent, "Ah, there he goes with his two goats; if he slits their throats, he may have more peace of mind." "What has he to worry about anyway? They live on nothing and have none to worry about." Thus people commented when he passed through the village. Only on the outskirts did he lift his head and look up. He urged and bullied the goats until they meandered along to the foot of the horse statue on the edge of the village. He sat on its pedestal for the rest of the day. The advantage of this was that he could watch the highway and see the lorries and buses pass through to the hills, and it gave him a sense of belonging to a larger world. The pedestal of the statue was broad enough for him to move around as the sun travelled up and westward; or he could also crouch under the belly of the horse, for shade.

The horse was nearly life-size, moulded out of clay, baked, burnt, and brightly coloured, and reared its head proudly, prancing its forelegs in the air and flourishing its tail in a loop; beside the horse stood a warrior with scythe-like mustachios, bulging eyes, and aquiline nose. The old image-makers believed in indicating a man of strength by bulging out his eyes and sharpening his moustache tips, and also decorated the man's chest with beads which looked to-day like blobs of mud through the ravages of sun and wind and rain (when it came), but Muni would insist that he had known the beads to sparkle like the nine gems at one time in his life. The horse itself was said to have been as white as a dhobi-washed sheet, and had had on its back a cover of pure brocade of red and black lace, matching the multicoloured sash around the waist of the warrior. But none in the village remembered the splendour as no one noticed its existence. Even Muni, who spent all his waking hours at its foot, never bothered to look up. It was untouched even by the young vandals of the village who gashed tree trunks with knives and tried to topple off milestones and inscribed lewd designs on all walls. This statue had been closer to the population of the village at one time, when this spot bordered the village; but when the highway was laid through (or perhaps when the tank and wells dried up completely here) the village moved a couple of miles inland.

Muni sat at the foot of the statue, watching his two goats graze in the arid soil among the cactus and lantana bushes. He looked at the sun; it had tilted westward no doubt, but it was not the time yet to go back home; if he went too early his wife would have no food for him. Also he must give her time to cool off her temper and feel sympathetic, and then she would scrounge and manage to get some food. He watched the mountain road for a time signal. When the green bus appeared around the bend he could leave, and his wife would feel pleased that he had let the goats feed long enough.

He noticed now a new sort of vehicle coming down at full speed. It looked like both a motor car and a bus. He used to be intrigued by the novelty of such spectacles, but of late work was going on at the source of the river on the mountain and an assortment of people and traffic went past him, and he took it all casually and described to his wife, later in the day, everything he saw. Today, while he observed the yellow vehicle coming down, he was wondering how to describe it later to his wife when it sputtered and stopped in front of him. A red-faced foreigner, who had been driving it, got down and went round it, stooping, looking, and poking under the vehicle; then he straightened himself up, looked at the dashboard, stared in Muni's direction, and approached him. "Excuse me, is there a gas station nearby, or do I have to wait until another car comes—" He suddenly looked up at the clay horse and cried, "Marvellous," without completing his sentence. Muni felt he should get up and run away, and cursed his age. He could not readily put his limbs into action; some years ago he could outrun a cheetah, as happened once when he went to the forest to cut fuel and it was then that two of his sheep were mauled—a sign that bad times were coming. Though he tried, he could not easily extricate himself from his seat, and then there was also the problem of the goats. He could not leave them behind.

The red-faced man wore khaki clothes—evidently a policeman or a soldier. Muni said to himself, "He will chase or shoot if I start running. Some dogs chase only those who run—oh, Shiva protect me. I don't know why this man should be after me." Meanwhile the foreigner cried, "Marvellous!" again, nodding his head. He paced around the statue with his eyes fixed on it. Muni sat frozen for a while, and then fidgeted and tried to edge away. Now the other man suddenly pressed his palms together in a salute, smiled, and said, "Namaste! How do you do?"

At which Muni spoke the only English expressions he had learnt, "Yes, no." Having exhausted his English vocabulary, he started in Tamil: "My name is Muni. These two goats are mine, and no one can gainsay it—though our village is full of slanderers these days who will not hesitate to say that what belongs to a man doesn't belong to him." He rolled his eyes and shuddered at the thought of evil-minded men and women peopling his village.

The foreigner faithfully looked in the direction indicated by Muni's fingers, gazed for a while at the two goats and the rocks, and with a puzzled expression took out his silver cigarette case and lit a cigarette. Suddenly remembering the courtesies of the season, he asked, "Do you smoke?" Muni answered, "Yes, no." Whereupon the red-faced man took a cigarette and gave it to Muni, who received it with surprise, having had no offer of a smoke from anyone for years now. Those days when he smoked bhang were gone with his sheep and the large-hearted butcher. Nowadays he was not able to find even matches, let alone bhang. (His wife went across and borrowed a fire at dawn from a neighbour.) He had always wanted to smoke a cigarette; only once did the shopman give him one on credit, and he remembered how good it had tasted. The other flicked the lighter open and offered a light to Muni. Muni felt so confused about how to act that he blew on it and put it out. The other, puzzled but undaunted, flourished his lighter, presented it again, and lit Muni's cigarette. Muni drew a deep puff and started coughing; it was racking, no doubt, but extremely pleasant. When his cough subsided he wiped his eyes and took stock of the situation, understanding that the other man was not an Inquisitor of any kind. Yet, in order to make sure, he remained wary. No need to run away from a man who gave him such a potent smoke. His head was reeling from the effect of one of those strong American cigarettes made with roasted tobacco. The man said, "I come from New York," took out a wallet from his hip pocket, and presented his card.

Muni shrank away from the card. Perhaps he was trying to present a warrant and arrest him. Beware of khaki, one part of his mind warned. Take all the cigarettes or bhang or whatever is offered, but don't get caught. Beware of khaki. He wished he weren't seventy as the shopman had said. At seventy one didn't run, but surrendered to whatever came. He could only ward off trouble by talk. So he went on, all in the chaste Tamil for which Kritam was famous. (Even the worst detractors could not deny that the famous poetess Avvaiyar was born in this area, although no one could say whether it was in Kritam or Kuppam, the adjoining village.) Out of this heritage the Tamil language gushed through Muni in an unimpeded flow. He said, "Before God, sir, Bhagwan, who sees everything, I tell you, sir, that we know nothing of the case. If the murder was committed, whoever did it will not escape. Bhagwan is all-seeing. Don't ask me about it. I know nothing." A body had been found mutilated and thrown under a tamarind tree at the border between Kritam and Kuppam a few weeks before, giving rise to much gossip and speculation. Muni added an explanation. "Anything is possible there. People over there will stop at nothing." The foreigner nodded his head and listened courteously though he understood nothing.

"I am sure you know when this horse was made," said the red man and smiled ingratiatingly.

Muni reacted to the relaxed atmosphere by smiling himself, and pleaded, "Please go away, sir, I know nothing. I promise we will hold him for you if we see any bad character around, and we will bury him up to his neck in a coconut pit if he tries to escape; but our village has always had a clean record. Must definitely be the other village."

Now the red man implored, "Please, please, I will speak slowly, please try to understand me. Can't you understand even a simple word of English? Everyone in this country seems to know English. I have gotten along with English everywhere in this country, but you don't speak it. Have you any religious or spiritual scruples against English speech?"

Muni made some indistinct sounds in his throat and shook his head. Encouraged, the other went on to explain at length, uttering each syllable with care and deliberation. Presently he sidled over and took a seat beside the old man, explaining, "You see, last August, we probably had the hottest summer in history, and I was working in shirt-sleeves in my office on the fortieth floor of the Empire State Building. We had a power failure one day, you know, and there I was stuck for four hours, no elevator, no air conditioning. All the way in the train I kept thinking, and the minute I reached home in Connecticut, I told my wife Ruth, 'We will visit India this winter, it's time to look at other civilizations.' Next day she called the travel agent first thing and told him to fix it, and so here I am. Ruth came with me but is staying back at Srinagar, and I am the one doing the rounds and joining her later."

Muni looked reflective at the end of this long oration and said, rather feebly, "Yes, no," as a concession to the other's language, and went on in Tamil, "When I was this high"—he indicated a foot high—"I had heard my uncle say . . ."

No one can tell what he was planning to say, as the other interrupted him at this stage to ask, "Boy, what is the secret of your teeth? How old are you?"

The old man forgot what he had started to say and remarked, "Sometimes we too lose our cattle. Jackals or cheetahs may sometimes carry them off, but sometimes it is just theft from over in the next village, and then we will know who has done it. Our priest at the temple can see in the camphor flame the face of the thief, and when he is caught . . ." He gestured with his hands a perfect mincing of meat.

The American watched his hands intently and said, "I know what you mean. Chop something? Maybe I am holding you up and you want to chop wood? Where is your axe? Hand it to me and show me what to chop. I do enjoy it, you know, just a hobby. We get a lot of driftwood along the backwater near my house, and on Sundays I do nothing but chop wood for the fireplace. I really feel different when I watch the fire in the fireplace, although it may take all the sections of the Sunday *New York Times* to get a fire started." And he smiled at this reference.

Muni felt totally confused but decided the best thing would be to make an attempt to get away from this place. He tried to edge out, saying, "Must go home," and turned to go. The other seized his shoulder and said desperately, "Is there no one, absolutely no one here, to translate for me?" He looked up and down the road, which was deserted in this hot afternoon; a sudden gust of wind churned up the dust and dead leaves on the roadside into a ghostly column and propelled it towards the mountain road. The stranger almost pinioned Muni's back to the statue and asked, "Isn't this statue yours? Why don't you sell it to me?"

The old man now understood the reference to the horse, thought for a second, and said in his own language, "I was an urchin this high when I heard my grandfather explain this horse and warrior, and my grandfather himself was this high when he heard his grandfather, whose grandfather . . ."

The other man interrupted him. "I don't want to seem to have stopped here for nothing. I will offer you a good price for this," he said, indicating the horse. He had concluded without the least doubt that Muni owned this mud horse. Perhaps he guessed by the way he sat on its pedestal, like other souvenir sellers in this country presiding over their wares.

Muni followed the man's eyes and pointing fingers and dimly understood the subject matter and, feeling relieved that the theme of the mutilated body had been abandoned at least for the time being, said again, enthusiastically, "I was this high when my grandfather told me about this horse and the warrior, and my grandfather was this high when he himself . . ." and he was getting into a deeper bog of reminiscence each time he tried to indicate the antiquity of the statue.

The Tamil that Muni spoke was stimulating even as pure sound, and the foreigner listened with fascination. "I wish I had my tape-recorder here," he said, assuming the pleasantest expression. "Your language sounds wonderful. I get a kick out of every word you utter, here"—he indicated his ears—"but you don't have to waste your breath in sales talk. I appreciate the article. You don't have to explain its points."

"I never went to a school, in those days only Brahmin went to schools, but we had to go out and work in the fields morning till night, from sowing to harvest time . . . and when Pongal came and we had cut the harvest, my father allowed me to go out and play with others at the tank, and so I don't know the Parangi language you speak, even little fellows in your country probably speak the Parangi language, but here only learned men and officers know it. We had a postman in our village who could speak to you boldly in your language, but his wife ran away with someone and he does not speak to anyone at all nowadays. Who would if a wife did what she did? Women must be watched; otherwise they will sell themselves and the home." And he laughed at his own quip.

The foreigner laughed heartily, took out another cigarette, and offered it to Muni, who now smoked with ease, deciding to stay on if the fellow was going to be so good as to keep up his cigarette supply. The American now stood up on the pedestal in the attitude of a demonstrative lecturer and said, running his finger along some of the carved decorations around the horse's neck, speaking slowly and uttering his words syllable by syllable, "I could give a sales talk for this better than anyone else. . . . This is a marvellous combination of yellow and indigo, though faded now. . . . How do you people of this country achieve these flaming colours?"

Muni, now assured that the subject was still the horse and not the dead body, said, "This is our guardian, it means death to our adversaries. At the end of Kali Yuga, this world and all other worlds will be destroyed, and the Redeemer will come in the shape of a horse called 'Kalki'; this horse will come to life and gallop and trample down all bad men." As he spoke of bad men the figures of his shopman and his brother-in-law assumed concrete forms in his mind, and he revelled for a moment in the predicament of the fellow under the horse's hoof: served him right for trying to set fire to his home. . . .

While he was brooding on this pleasant vision, the foreigner utilized the pause to say, "I assure you that this will have the best home in the U.S.A. I'll push away the bookcase, you know I love books and am a member of five book clubs, and the choice and bonus volumes mount up to a pile really in our living room, as high as this horse itself. But they'll have to go. Ruth may disapprove, but I will convince her. The T.V. may have to be shifted too. We can't have everything in the living room. Ruth will probably say what about when we have a party? I'm going to keep him right in the middle of the room. I don't see how that can interfere with the party—we'll stand around him and have our drinks."

Muni continued his description of the end of the world. "Our pundit discoursed at the temple once how the oceans are going to close over the earth in a huge wave and swallow us—this horse will grow bigger than the biggest wave and carry on its back only the good people and kick into the floods the evil ones—plenty of them about—" he said reflectively. "Do you know when it is going to happen?" he asked.

The foreigner now understood by the tone of the other that a question was being asked and said, "How am I transporting it? I can push the seat back and make room in the rear. That van can take in an elephant"—waving precisely at the back of the seat.

Muni was still hovering on visions of avatars and said again, "I never missed our pundit's discourses at the temple in those days during every bright half of the month, although he'd go on all night, and he told us that Vishnu is the highest god. Whenever evil men trouble us, he comes down to save us. He has come many times. The first time he incarnated as a great fish, and lifted the scriptures on his back when the floods and sea waves . . ."

"I am not a millionaire, but a modest businessman. My trade is coffee."

Amidst all this wilderness of obscure sound Muni caught the word "coffee" and said, "If you want to drink 'kapi,' drive further up, in the next town, they have Friday market, and there they open 'kapi-otels'—so I learn from passers-by. Don't think I wander about. I go nowhere and look for nothing." His thoughts went back to the avatars. "The first avatar was in the shape of a little fish in a bowl of water, but every hour it grew bigger and bigger and became in the end a huge whale which the seas could not contain, and on the back of the whale the holy books were supported, saved and carried." Once he had launched on the first avatar, it was inevitable that he should go on to the next, a wild boar on whose tusk the earth was lifted when a vicious conqueror of the earth carried it off and hid it at the bottom of the sea. After describing this avatar Muni concluded, "God will always save us whenever we are troubled by evil beings. When we were young we staged at full moon the story of the avatars. That's how I know the stories; we played them all night until the sun rose, and sometimes the European collector would come to watch, bringing his own chair. I had a good voice and so they always taught me songs and gave me the women's roles. I was always Goddess Lakshmi, and they dressed me in a brocade sari, loaned from the Big House . . ."

The foreigner said, "I repeat I am not a millionaire. Ours

is a modest business; after all, we can't afford to buy more than sixty minutes of T.V. time in a month, which works out to two minutes a day, that's all, although in the course of time we'll maybe sponsor a one-hour show regularly if our sales graph continues to go up . . ."

Muni was intoxicated by the memory of his theatrical days and was about to explain how he had painted his face and worn a wig and diamond earrings when the visitor, feeling that he had spent too much time already, said, "Tell me, will you accept a hundred rupees or not for the horse? I'd love to take the whiskered soldier also but no space for him this year. I'll have to cancel my air ticket and take a boat home, I suppose. Ruth can go by air if she likes, but I will go with the horse and keep him in my cabin all the way if necessary." And he smiled at the picture of himself voyaging across the seas hugging this horse. He added, "I will have to pad it with straw so that it doesn't break . . ."

"When we played *Ramayana,* they dressed me as Sita," added Muni. "A teacher came and taught us the songs for the drama and we gave him fifty rupees. He incarnated himself as Rama, and He alone could destroy Ravana, the demon with ten heads who shook all the worlds; do you know the story of *Ramayana?*"

"I have my station wagon as you see. I can push the seat back and take the horse in if you will just lend me a hand with it."

"Do you know *Mahabharata?* Krishna was the eighth avatar of Vishnu, incarnated to help the Five Brothers regain their kingdom. When Krishna was a baby he danced on the thousand-hooded giant serpent and trampled it to death; and then he suckled the breasts of the demoness and left them flat as a disc though when she came to him her bosoms were large, like mounds of earth on the banks of a dug up canal." He indicated two mounds with his hands. The stranger was completely mystified by the gesture. For the first time he said, "I really wonder what you are saying because your answer is crucial. We have come to the point when we should be ready to talk business."

"When the tenth avatar comes, do you know where you and I will be?" asked the old man.

"Lend me a hand and I can lift off the horse from its pedestal after picking out the cement at the joints. We can do anything if we have a basis of understanding."

At this stage the mutual mystification was complete, and there was no need even to carry on a guessing game at the meaning of words. The old man chattered away in a spirit of balancing off the credits and debits of conversational exchange, and said in order to be on the credit side, "Oh, honourable one, I hope God has blessed you with numerous progeny. I say this because you seem to be a good man, willing to stay beside an old man and talk to him, while all day I have none to talk to except when somebody stops by to ask for a piece of tobacco. But I seldom have it, tobacco is not what it used to be at one time, and I have given up chewing. I cannot afford it nowadays." Noting the other's interest in his speech, Muni felt encouraged to ask, "How many children have you?" with appropriate gestures with his hands. Realizing that a question was being asked, the red man replied, "I said a hundred," which encouraged Muni to go into details. "How many of your children are boys and how many girls? Where are they? Is your daughter married? Is it difficult to find a son-in-law in your country also?"

In answer to these questions the red man dashed his hand

into his pocket and brought forth his wallet in order to take immediate advantage of the bearish trend in the market. He flourished a hundred-rupee currency note and said, "Well, this is what I meant."

The old man now realized that some financial element was entering their talk. He peered closely at the currency note, the like of which he had never seen in his life; he knew the five and ten by their colours although always in other people's hands, while his own earning at any time was in coppers and nickels. What was this man flourishing the note for? Perhaps asking for change. He laughed to himself at the notion of anyone coming to him for changing a thousand- or ten-thousand-rupee note. He said with a grin, "Ask our village headman, who is also a moneylender; he can change even a lakh of rupees in gold sovereigns if you prefer it that way; he thinks nobody knows, but dig the floor of his puja room and your head will reel at the sight of the hoard. The man disguises himself in rags just to mislead the public. Talk to the headman yourself because he goes mad at the sight of me. Someone took away his pumpkins with the creeper and he, for some reason, thinks it was me and my goats . . . that's why I never let my goats be seen anywhere near the farms." His eyes travelled to his goats nosing about, attempting to wrest nutrition from minute greenery peeping out of rock and dry earth.

The foreigner followed his look and decided that it would be a sound policy to show an interest in the old man's pets. He went up casually to them and stroked their backs with every show of courteous attention. Now the truth dawned on the old man. His dream of a lifetime was about to be realized. He understood that the red man was actually making an offer for the goats. He had reared them up in the hope of selling them some day and, with the capital, opening a small shop on this very spot. Sitting here, watching towards the hills, he had often dreamt how he would put up a thatched roof here, spread a gunny sack out on the ground, and display on it fried nuts, coloured sweets, and green coconut for the thirsty and famished wayfarers on the highway, which was sometimes very busy. The animals were not prize ones for a cattle show, but he had spent his occasional savings to provide them some fancy diet now and then, and they did not look too bad. While he was reflecting thus, the red man shook his hand and left on his palm one hundred rupees in tens now, suddenly realizing that this was what the old man was asking. "It is all for you or you may share it if you have a partner."

The old man pointed at the station wagon and asked, "Are you carrying them off in that?"

"Yes, of course," said the other, understanding the transportation part of it.

The old man said, "This will be their first ride in a motor car. Carry them off after I get out of sight, otherwise they will never follow you, but only me even if I am travelling on the path to Yama Loka." He laughed at his own joke, brought his palms together in a salute, turned round and went off, and was soon out of sight beyond a clump of thicket.

The red man looked at the goats grazing peacefully. Perched on the pedestal of the horse, as the westerly sun touched off the ancient faded colours of the statue with a fresh splendour, he ruminated, "He must be gone to fetch some help, I suppose!" and settled down to wait. When a truck came downhill, he stopped it and got the help of a couple of men to detach the horse from its pedestal and place it in his station wagon. He gave them five rupees each, and for a further payment they siphoned off gas from the truck, and helped him to start his engine.

Muni hurried homeward with the cash securely tucked away at his waist in his dhoti. He shut the street door and stole up softly to his wife as she squatted before the lit oven wondering if by a miracle food would drop from the sky. Muni displayed his fortune for the day. She snatched the notes from him, counted them by the glow of the fire, and cried, "One hundred rupees! How did you come by it? Have you been stealing?"

"I have sold our goats to a red-faced man. He was absolutely crazy to have them, gave me all this money and carried them off in his motor car!"

Hardly had these words left his lips when they heard bleating outside. She opened the door and saw the two goats at her door. "Here they are!" she said. "What's the meaning of all this?"

He muttered a great curse and seized one of the goats by its ears and shouted, "Where is that man? Don't you know you are his? Why did you come back?" The goat only wriggled in his grip. He asked the same question of the other too. The goat shook itself off. His wife glared at him and declared, "If you have thieved, the police will come tonight and break your bones. Don't involve me. I will go away to my parents. . . ."

Uncle

I am the monarch of all I survey, being the sole occupant of this rambling ancient house in Vinayak Street. I am five-ten, too huge for the easy chair on which I am reclining now. But I remember the time when I could hardly reach the arm of this easy chair. I remember the same chair at the same spot in the hall, with some ancient portrait hanging on a nail over it, with my uncle comfortably lounging and tormenting me by pushing his glittering snuffbox just out of my reach. While trying to reach for it I tumbled down again and again; he emitted a loud guffaw each time I lost my balance and sprawled on the floor. I felt frightened by his loud laughter and whined and cried. At that moment my aunt would swoop down on me and carry me off to the kitchen, set me down in a corner, and place before me a little basin filled with water, which I splashed about. I needed no further attention except a replenishment of water from time to time. I also watched with wonderment the smoke curling up from the oven when the lady puffed her cheeks and blew on the fire through a hollow bamboo pipe. The spell would suddenly be broken when she picked me up again, with a bowl of rice in her hand, and carried me off to the street door. She would carefully seat me on the pyol of the house, my back supported against the slender pillars, and try to feed me. If I averted my head she gripped my neck as in a vise and forced the rice between my lips. If I howled in protest she utilized the chance to thrust more rice into my open mouth. If I spat it out she would point at a passer-by and say, "See that demon, he will carry you off. He is on the lookout for babies who won't eat." At that stage I must have faced the risk of dying of over rather than under-feeding. Later in the day she would place a dish of eatables before me and watch me deal with it. When I turned the dish over on the floor and messed up the contents, Uncle and Aunt drew each other's attention to this marvellous spectacle and nearly danced around me in joy. In those days my uncle, though portly as ever, possessed greater agility, I believe.

My uncle stayed at home all day. I was too young to consider what he did for a living. The question never occurred to me until I was old enough to sit on a school bench and discuss life's problems with a class fellow. I was studying in the first year at Albert Mission School. Our teacher had written on the blackboard a set of words such as Man, Dog, Cat, Mat, Taj, and Joy, and had asked us to copy them down on our slates and take them to him for correction and punishment if necessary. I had copied four of the six terms and had earned the teacher's approbation. The boy in the next seat had also done well. Our duties for the hour were over, and that left us free to talk, in subdued whispers, though.

"What is your father's name?" he asked.

"I don't know. I call him Uncle."

"Is he rich?" the boy asked.

"I don't know," I replied. "They make plenty of sweets at home."

"Where does he work?" asked the boy, and the first thing I did when I went home, even before flinging off my books and school bag, was to ask loudly, "Uncle, where is your office?"

He replied, "Up above," pointing heavenward, and I looked up.

"Are you rich?" was my second question.

My aunt emerged from the kitchen and dragged me in, saying, "Come, I have some very lovely things for you to eat."

I felt confused and asked my aunt, "Why won't Uncle . . . ?" She merely covered my mouth with her palm and warned, "Don't talk of all that."

"Why?" I asked.

"Uncle doesn't liked to be asked questions."

"I will not ask hereafter," I said and added, "Only that Suresh, he is a bad boy and he said . . ."

"Hush," she said.

My world was circumscribed by the boundaries of our house in Vinayak Street, and peopled by Uncle and Aunt mainly. I had no existence separately from my uncle. I clung to him all through the day. Mornings in the garden at the back yard, afternoons inside, and all evening on the front pyol of the house squatting beside him. When he prayed or meditated at midday I sat in front of him watching his face and imitating him. When he saw me mutter imaginary prayers with my eyes shut, he became ecstatic and cried aloud to my aunt in the kitchen, "See this fellow, how well he prays! We must teach him some slokas. No doubt whatever, he is going to be a saint someday. What do you think?" When he prostrated to the gods in the puja room I too threw myself on the floor, encouraged by the compliments showered on me. He would stand staring at me until Aunt reminded him that his lunch was ready. When he sat down to eat I nestled close to him, pressing my elbow on his lap. Aunt would say, "Move off, little man. Let Uncle eat in peace," but he always countermanded her and said, "Stay, stay." After lunch he chewed betel leaves and areca nut, moved on to his bedroom, and stretched himself on his rosewood bench, with a small pillow under his head. Just when he fell into a doze I demanded, "Tell me a story," butting him with my elbow.

He pleaded, "Let us both sleep. We may have wonderful dreams. After that I will tell you a story."

"What dreams?" I would persist.

"Shut your eyes and don't talk, and you will get nice dreams." And while I gave his advice a trial, he closed his eyes.

All too brief a trial. I cried, "No, I don't see any dream yet. Tell me a story, Uncle." He patted my head and murmured, "Once upon a time . . ." with such a hypnotic effect that within a few minutes I fell asleep.

Sometimes I sought a change from the stories and involved him in a game. The bench on which he tried to sleep would be a mountain top, the slight gap between its edge and the wall a gorge with a valley below. I would crawl under the bench, lie on my back, and command, "Now throw," having first heaped at his side a variety of articles such as a flashlight without battery, a ping-pong bat, a sandalwood incense holder, a leather wallet, a coat hanger, empty bottles, a tiny stuffed cow, and several other items out of a treasure chest I possessed. And over went the most cherished objects—the more fragile the better for the game, for, in the cool semidark world under the bench and by the rules of the game, the possibility of a total annihilation of objects would be perfectly in order.

Ten days after first broaching the subject Suresh cornered me again when we were let off for an hour in the absence of our geography master. We were playing marbles. Suresh suddenly said, "My father knows your uncle."

I felt uneasy. But I had not learnt the need for circumspection and asked anxiously, "What does he say about him?"

"Your uncle came from another country, a far-off place . . ."

"Oh, good, so?" I cried with happiness, feeling relieved that after all some good points about my uncle were emerging.

Suresh said, "But he impersonated."

"What is 'impersonate'?" I asked.

He said, "Something not so good. My mother and father were talking, and I heard them use the word."

The moment I came home from school and flung off my bag my aunt dragged me to the well in the back yard and forced me to wash my hands and feet, although I squirmed and protested vehemently. Next I sat on the arm of my uncle's easy chair with a plate filled with delicacies, ever available under that roof, and ate under the watchful eye of my uncle. Nothing delighted him more than to eat or watch someone eat. "What is the news in your school today?" he would ask.

"Know what happened, Uncle?" I swallowed a mouthful

and took time to suppress the word "impersonate," which kept welling up from the depths of my being, and invent a story. "A bad boy from the Third B—big fellow—jabbed me with his elbow . . ."

"Did he? Were you hurt?"

"Oh, no, he came charging but I stepped aside and he banged his head against the wall, and it was covered with blood, and they carried him to the hospital." My uncle uttered many cries of joy at the fate overtaking my adversary and induced me to develop the details, which always sounded gory.

When they let me go I bounced off to the street, where a gang awaited my arrival. We played marbles or kicked a rubber ball about with war cries and shouts, blissfully unaware of the passers-by and the traffic, until the street end melted into a blaze of luminous dust with the sun gone. We played until my uncle appeared at our doorway and announced, "Time to turn in," when we dispersed unceremoniously and noisily. Once again my aunt would want to give my hands and feet a scrubbing. "How many times!" I protested. "Won't I catch a cold at this rate?"

She just said, "You have all the road dust on you now. Come on." After dousing me she smeared sacred ash on my forehead and made me sit with my uncle in the back verandah of the house and recite holy verse. After which I picked up my school books and, under my uncle's supervision, read my lessons, both the tutor and the taught feeling exhausted at the end of it. By eight-thirty I would be fed and put to sleep in a corner of the hall, at the junction of the two walls where I felt most secure.

On Fridays we visited the little shrine at the end of our

street. Rather an exciting outing for me, as we passed along brilliantly lit shops displaying banana bunches, coloured drinks, bottled peppermints, and red and yellow paper kites, every item seeming to pulsate with an inner glow.

They both rose at five in the morning and moved about softly so as not to disturb me. The first thing in the day, my uncle drew water from the well for the family, and then watered the plants in the garden. I woke to the sound of the pulley creaking over the well and joined my uncle in the garden. In the morning light he looked like a magician. One asked for nothing more in life than to be up at that hour and watch brilliant eddying columns of water coming through little channels dug along the ground. The hydraulic engineering for the garden was my uncle's own. He had raised the ground beside the well to form a basin, and when he tipped a cauldron of water over it, the column ran down the slope and passed through to the plants according to his dictates. He controlled the supply of water at various stages with a little trowel in hand, with which he scooped up the mud and opened or blocked the water course. I floated little bits of straw or leaves, or picked up ants and helped them have a free swim along the current. Sometimes without my uncle's knowledge I scooped off the mud bank with my hands and diverted the water elsewhere.

I revelled in this world of mud, greens, slush, and water, forgetting for the moment such things as homework and teachers. When the sun came over the walls of the house behind our garden, my uncle ended his operations, poured a great quantity of water over himself, and went in dripping, in search of a towel. When I tried to follow him in, my aunt brought out a bucket of hot water and gave me a bath beside the well. Soon I found myself in the puja room murmuring prayers.

A perpetual smell of incense and flowers hung about the puja room, which was actually an alcove in the kitchen where pictures of gods hung on the walls. I loved the pictures; the great god Krishna poised on the hood of a giant serpent; Vishnu, blue-coloured, seated on the back of Garuda, the divine eagle, gliding in space and watching us. As I watched the pictures my mind went off into fantastic speculations while my tongue recited holy verse. "Was the eagle a sort of aeroplane for Vishnu? Lakshmi stands on lotus! How can anyone stand on a lotus flower without crushing it?" From the fireplace would come my aunt's voice, "I don't hear you pray." I would suppress my speculations and recite aloud, addressing the elephant-faced god, *"Gajananam bhutaganadi sevitam . . ."* for three minutes in Sanskrit. I always wanted to ask for its meaning, but if I paused my aunt would shout over the hissing of the frying pan (which, incidentally, was generating an enormously appetizing fragrance), "Why have you stopped?" Now I would turn to the picture of Saraswati, the goddess of learning, as she sat on a rock with her peacock beside a cool shrubbery, and wonder at her ability to play the veena with one hand while turning the rosary with the other, still leaving two hands free, perhaps to pat the peacock. I would raise my voice and say, *"Saraswati namastubhyam,"* which meant "O goddess of learning, I bow to you," or some such thing. I secretly added a personal request to this prayer. "May you help me get through my school hours without being mauled by my teachers or other boys, may I get through this day unscathed." Although my normal day at

school was peaceful, I always approached it at the beginning of each day with dread. My teacher was unshaven and
looked villainous. He frequently inhaled a pinch of snuff in
the class and spoke in a grating voice, the snuff having rav-
aged his vocal cords, and he flourished a short, stubby cane
menacingly at the whole class every now and then. I had
never seen him attack anyone, but his gestures were frightening, and I sat on my bench shuddering lest he should turn
in my direction and notice me.

My life was precisely organized by my uncle, and I had
little time to waste. When I emerged from the puja I had to
go straight to the kitchen and drink off a glass of milk. This
would be an occasion for my aunt to comment on my dress
or voice. She would suddenly bring her face close to mine
and examine my eyes. "What are you looking for?" I would
ask, rearing my head, but she held it firmly between her
palms and inspected until she was satisfied that there was no
patch of dirt or swelling under my eyes. "Oh, I was mistaken, nothing," she would say with relief. "Anyway, you
have grown darker. You must not roast yourself in the sun
so much. Why should they make you do all that drill in the
sun?"

Next I passed into the jurisdiction of my uncle, who sat
leaning against a pillar in the hall with eyes shut in meditation. He said, emerging from his trance, "Boy, gather all
your lessons for the day and put them in your bag. Have you
sharpened your pencil? Cleaned your slate? Do you need
anything?" In spite of my firm statement that I needed
nothing, he came over, seized my school bag, peered into it,
and probed its bottom with his fingers. It was surprising
how lightly he could abandon his prayers, but he was perhaps an adept who could resume them at will, as his day was

mostly divided between munching and meditation. He held up to the light a slate pencil in order to judge whether it could be used for just another day. He would sharpen its point on the stone floor, commenting, "You must hold it here and write, and don't bite the end; this can be used for a week more." It was painful to write with such a short stub; my thumb and forefinger became sore, and further, if my teacher noticed it he twisted my ear and snatched away the stub and made me stand on the bench as a punishment. I could not mention these problems explicitly, as I feared that my uncle might don his shirt and offer to visit my school in order to investigate. I had a secret anxiety lest he should ever appear in our school, as I thought that the boys might stand around and make fun of his girth. And so I had to manage with the stub as ordained. When he felt satisfied that I had used the pencil wisely, he would open his wooden cupboard, take out a lacquered casket with a dragon on its lid, and out of it a small cardboard box, and again from it a little package containing long slate pencils. He would take out a brand-new one and hesitate; guessing his intention, I would jump up and snatch it from his hand crying, "Don't break it, I want it full-length." Sometimes he gave it whole, sometimes he broke it into two saying, "Half is long enough." He then looked through my books page by page, and packed them securely back into the bag. He said from time to time, "Little man, if you don't read your lessons properly you will never count for anything in life and no one will respect you. Do you understand?" "Yes, Uncle," I said though not very clear in my mind as to what "respect" meant.

One evening I came home announcing, "They are going to photograph us in our school." My uncle, who had been lounging in the easy chair, sprang to his feet and asked, "Who? Who is going to photograph you?"

"My teacher's brother has a friend who has a camera and he is going to photograph us."

"Only you or others also?"

"Our class alone, not even the B section will be allowed, although they asked to be photographed too."

Uncle's face lit up with joy. He called Aunt and said, "Did you hear, this young man is going to be photographed tomorrow. Dress him properly."

Next day my uncle spent a lot of time selecting clothes for me, and my aunt gave a double rub to my face and groomed me. My uncle followed me about uttering several pieces of advice before letting me out. "You must never scowl even if the sun hits you in the eyes. You must try to look pleasant. You know in those days only girls waiting to be married used to have their photos taken. Nowadays everyone is being photographed."

When I came home from school that evening he asked anxiously, "How did it go off?"

I flung away the school bag to its corner and said, "No, nothing happened. He didn't come."

"Who?"

"Our teacher's brother's friend," I said. "It seems his camera has broken down or something like that, and so— no photo."

My uncle's face fell. Both of them had been waiting at the door to see me return triumphantly from the photographer. He murmured sympathetically, "Don't worry about it, we will find another photographer; only I thought you should not have taken out the blue shirt until Deepavali—never mind; we will buy you a new one for the festival."

My aunt said, "We could fold the shirt neatly and put it away until Deepavali. He has not soiled it."

"I sat very quietly today lest the clothes should be spoilt," I said, which was a fact. I had refused to play with my friends for fear that my shirt might get crumpled. This blue shirt was of a special kind; my uncle had bought the cloth from a street hawker, who assured him that the fabric was foreign and could not normally be acquired except through smugglers operating in certain coastal villages. Uncle bought three yards of the blue cloth after a whole afternoon's haggling, and planned to stitch shirts for me and himself. He had sent for an old Muslim tailor who had the original Singer sewing machine set up on the pyol of a house in Kabir Lane. He behaved extremely deferentially before my uncle and would not be seated even on the floor. My uncle relaxed in his easy chair and my aunt stood at the kitchen doorway and both discussed with the tailor various matters relating to persons, times, and places which sounded remote and incomprehensible to me. He kept addressing my uncle as his saviour at the end of every sentence, and salaamed him. When the time came to take measurements my uncle stood very erect and muttered numerous instructions as to the length, cut, and number and kind (unbreakable, tin) of buttons that he favoured, and so forth. "Note the measurements down properly," he said sternly several times, "lest you should forget and make a mistake; it is a rare kind of cloth, not obtainable in our country; can't afford to take chances with it, remember."

The tailor in answer avowed again his indebtedness to my uncle. "On the road that day if you had not—" he began.

My uncle looked embarrassed and cut him short with, "Don't go on with all those grandmother's stories now. The past is past, remember."

"How can I help it, sir? Every morning I and my children think of you and pray for your welfare. When they gave me up for dead with vultures circling above and passed on, you stopped by and revived me, sir, although you had this baby in your arms . . . and you gave me the strength to walk a thousand miles over mountain passes. . . ."

My uncle said curtly, "Why don't you take the measurements?"

"I obey," said the tailor immediately, and proceeded to measure me. He was not only deferential but also patronizing in his tone. "Stand up, little master, otherwise you will blame this old man for any mistake that may occur. See how your venerable uncle stands erect at his age!"

He completed the measurements, noted them on a very small roll of paper, probably the torn-off margin of a newspaper, with a stubby pencil which he always carried over his ear, and departed after accepting all the advice given as they kept saying, "Remember he is a growing boy, make allowance for that; don't want him to feel suffocated in his new shirt after the first wash . . ."

The tailor left after uttering the only word of protest, "If master had bought just a quarter yard more . . ."

"Not at all necessary," said my uncle. "I know how much is needed, seeing that you are going to give me short arms, and no collar is wanted. . . ." The shirts came back stitched in due course and were laid away in the big trunk.

Next evening I came home gleefully announcing, "We were photographed today."

"Indeed!" cried my uncle. "How stupid of them when you were not ready for it!"

"Does it mean that you are going to look like this in the photo?" asked my aunt.

"It will not do justice to you," said my uncle. "They should have given us at least half an hour's notice, and then you could have . . ."

"Our teacher suddenly said, 'Come out, all of you, and stand in a line under the tree.' We marched out. A man came with a small camera, lined up all the tall boys first and all the short ones in the second line with our teacher in the centre; and then he cried, 'Stand steady, don't move,' and it was over. Our teacher has promised to give a photo to whoever brings two rupees from home."

"Two rupees!" repeated my uncle aghast.

Aunt said, "Never mind, it is the child's first photo."

"I thought the class would be let off after the photo, but we were marched back for geography lessons."

My uncle thrust two rupees into my pocket before I left for school next day, cautioning me, "Take it carefully to your teacher." He sounded anxious lest I should drop the money or get robbed on the way. He stood on the front step and watched me go. I turned around a couple of times to assure him, "Don't fear. I will be careful," dreading lest he should suddenly don his shirt and decide to escort me.

For two weeks there was no sign of the photo. My uncle got quite agitated and asked every day, "What did your teacher say?" I had to invent an answer each time as I did not have the courage to confront my teacher on the subject. And so I generally said, "The photographer has been very ill. But tomorrow positively we are getting it."

Ultimately the photo did arrive and we were given our copies at the end of the day. As I reached home I shouted from the street, "Photo!" which brought my uncle down the steps of the house. He followed me anxiously about while I took my own time to fish out the photograph from my school bag. "Such a small one!" my uncle cried on seeing it.

"His camera also was small!" I said.

They carried the print to a corner where a beam of sunlight streamed in through the red pane of a ventilator and observed it closely. Uncle put his spectacles on, but my aunt had to wait for her turn since they managed with a single pair between them. "Why can't we go out, it is brighter out there, and I won't need glasses?" she suggested.

"No," he replied firmly. "Inquisitive fellows all around —fellows ready to peer through the wall if they could, to learn what is happening here," said my uncle, passing on his spectacles and commenting, "Our boy has the brightest face in the group, but they have made him look so dark!"

I pointed out my enemies to them: "This is Suresh— always trying to kill me if I am not careful. This boy also is a bad fellow." My aunt's eyes met mine significantly at the mention of Suresh, who looked florid by the red light of the ventilator. "This is our teacher. He will not hesitate to skin alive anyone who is found talking in his class. The man who took the photo is his brother's friend. Own brother, not cousin. Suresh asked if he was a cousin, and it made my teacher so wild!"

My uncle counted the heads and cried, "Fifty? Two rupees each and they have collected their one hundred rupees! Not even a mount for the photo! They are robbing us in your schools nowadays!"

Next day when I was leaving for school my uncle said, "Come home early. We will go out to the market. Have you any important lessons?"

"No, none," I said with conviction. "I will come home for lunch and stay on."

"Do you wish to come with us?" he asked, aiming his question in the direction of his wife in the kitchen. My aunt, with her years of experience behind her, flung back the responsibility of a decision on him, shouting from the fireplace, "Do you want me to go with you?" The man was cornered now and answered, "Not if you have things to mind at home . . ."

"Of course, I have asked that servant woman to come and pound the paddy today. If we miss her today she will not come again." She trailed off indecisively. This was a diplomatic game which, in spite of my age of innocence, I understood very well, and so I broke in, "Let Aunt come another day, Uncle. She will want a carriage to be brought and all that trouble," which was a fact, whenever she wanted to go out she would send me running to the street corner to fetch a jutka, and it was not always an easy job. Some days you found six jutkas waiting for fares under the margosa shade at the street corner, some days you couldn't find even one at a busy hour; sometimes the jutka drivers who knew me would tease and not take me seriously or pass disparaging remarks about my uncle, referring to him as "that Rangoon man" or mention incidents which I could not comprehend, and generally mumble and smirk among themselves at my expense.

My uncle added, "Quite right. We can walk to the market."

"Yes, by all means," said my aunt, much to everyone's relief.

We sallied out at three o'clock in the afternoon, having finished our tiffin and coffee. The main job for the day was to mount and frame the photograph. Uncle carried it in his hand delicately, enclosed in an old envelope, as if it were fragile and likely to perish at a finger's pressure. As we went down the street a neighbour standing at his door hailed us and demanded, "Where are you taking the young fellow?" He was an engineer who worked in some distant projects on the hills, coming home once in a while and then again disappearing from our society. He was a particular friend of my uncle as they occasionally gathered for a game of cards in my house. He asked, "I am here for a few days, can't we have a session sometime?"

"Of course, of course," said my uncle without much fervour, "I will let you know," and moved on.

"Won't aunt get angry?" I asked, remembering the arguments they had had after every card session. The card players would have been sitting around in the middle of the hall, demanding coffee and edibles, and playing far into the night. My aunt would complain after the company had dispersed, "Sitting there with your friends, you lock me up in the kitchen all day! What madness seizes you people when you touch a pack of cards, I wonder!" Worn out by her attacks, my uncle began to avoid his friends, the company gradually dwindled and disappeared. But it did not prevent them from dreaming about cards or luxuriating in visions of a grand session. Somewhere my uncle was supposed to have lost a lot of money through the card games, and my aunt was very definite that he should never go near cards again, although he kept saying, "We play only Twenty-eight, and not Rummy, after all, Twenty-eight . . ."

"Twenty-eight or forty-eight, it's all the same to me," said my aunt. "Fifty thousand rupees just scattered like waste paper, that is all! Sheer madness!" She was rather emphatic. My uncle, not being a quarrelsome sort, just accepted meekly whatever she said, and evidently benefited by her advice.

As we walked on I asked many questions. This was my opportunity to clear my doubts and learn about new things in life. I asked, "Why does not Aunt like playing cards? So many nice people gather in our house and it is so interesting!"

He answered, "It is very expensive, my boy, some people have lost all their fortune and become beggars. Gambling is bad. Don't you know how Nala lost his kingdom?" And he began to narrate the ancient story of Nala. Cyclists passed, a herd of cattle returned from the grazing fields beyond the river, some very young school children emerged from the town primary school, the sun scorching us all. But my uncle noticed nothing while he unfolded to me the fate of Nala, holding me by the wrist lest I should be run over or gored by the cattle. I shrank behind him when we passed my school. I had skipped three classes in the afternoon and did not wish to be seen by my teachers or classmates. We could hear the voices from within the classrooms. Presently the bell for the three-thirty recess would sound and the boys would rush out to drink water at the tap or to make water on the roadside or swarm around the groundnut seller at

the school gate. The headmaster was likely to prowl about
to prevent the boys from fouling the road. It would be disaster for me to be seen by anyone now. Nor did I wish my
uncle to get any ideas while passing the gate—such as stopping to have a word with my teacher. I quickened my steps
and tried to divert his mind to other matters by suddenly
saying, "Why did Nala lose?"

Before answering he paused for a moment to ask, "Is that
noise all from your school? Why do they make all that row?
Glad we don't live next door to your school!" Not wanting
him to dwell too much on school matters, I trotted ahead of
him, hoping to set the pace for him. But he remarked, "Do
you have to caper like that? No, my boy, I could have given
you a beating five years ago, but today I am deliberately
slowing my pace." I paused for him to catch up with me. We
had crossed the danger zone, gone past the school.

I asked innocently as we resumed our march, "What
game did Nala play? Did he play cards?"

"Oh, no," uncle said, "I am sure he would have, if they
had invented playing cards in those days. He played dice."
He went on to explain the game to me and continued the
story. "The fellow played with his brother, but malevolent
gods had got into the dice and affected his chances, and he
lost his kingdom and everything except his wife and had to
march out of the capital like a mendicant wearing only a
loin cloth."

We turned to our right and took a short cut through
Kabir Street and were on Market Road. Not a busy hour, as
the high-school boys were still not let off. Several donkeys
stood about the fountain statuesquely. When the boys
emerged from the high school, I imagined, they would

shout and frighten the donkeys, provoke them in various ways until they ran helter-skelter, confusing the evening traffic. Street dogs dozing on the edge of the road would join the fray and give them a chase, and there would be a hullabaloo. I missed all this imagined spectacle and told my uncle, "We should have come a little later."

"Why?" asked my uncle and added, "You wish that you had attended your classes after all?"

"Oh, no," I said, and blurted out, "We could have seen the donkeys jump about." Even without this spectacle, Market Road thrilled me every inch, so full of life, movement, and activity. A candy peddler was crying his wares, sounding a bell. This man often established himself at our school gate, drawing out and pinching off portions of a pink, elastic, gluey sweet, stuck in a coil around a bamboo shaft. My mouth watered at the sight of it. I pleaded, "Uncle, please get me a bit of it!"

He suddenly looked serious and said, "No, no, it is dangerous to eat such stuff. You may catch cholera."

I said with bravado, "Not likely. He comes to our school every day, and all boys eat it, and also our drawing master. No one has suffered from cholera yet."

All that he said was, "I will get you something nicer to eat. Wait." As we passed a sweetmeat shop he said, "This is Jagan's shop. No harm in eating here. He makes things out of pure ghee." He stopped by a resplendently arrayed sweetmeat shop and bought a packet for me.

I swiftly unpacked it and asked out of courtesy, "Uncle, you want some?" and when he shook his head I ate it, and threw away the wrapper high up and watched it gently float down on Market Road until Uncle pulled me up, saying, "Look in front and walk."

The frame-maker's name was Jayraj. He had hoisted a signboard which was rather pompously worded "Photographers & Photo-framers," stretching the entire width of the outer wall of the market. Why he chose to display himself in the plural no one could say, since no one ever saw anyone except Mr. Jayraj in the proprietor's seat in the inner sanctum. Although there was always a goodly company on the long bench sticking out from his threshold, they were all his friends, well-wishers, customers, and general listeners as Jayraj held forth on his social and personal philosophy all day. Now he gestured to us to be seated on the bench while he went on gently hammering tacks onto the sides of a frame covered with a cardboard. Presently he looked up and greeted my uncle, "Doctor, where have you been all these days?"

I was surprised at my uncle being addressed as a doctor. Immediately I looked up and asked, "Uncle, are you a doctor?" He merely rumpled my hair and did not answer.

Jayraj took this occasion to look at me and say, "Brought this young man along, who is he?"

My uncle simply said, "He is my boy, our child at home."

"Oh, I know, yes of course, now grown up so!"

My uncle looked slightly awkward and changed the subject. He held out my photograph and asked with affected cheer, "Oh, here is this young man's photo which must be framed. Will you do it?"

"Of course, anything for you, sir." He looked at the photo with disgust. I thought he might fling the picture into the gutter that flowed copiously below the steps of his shop. His brow was furrowed, he pursed his lips, blinked his eyes, placed a straight finger across the picture, shook his head dolefully, and said, "This is how people cheat schoolboys nowadays. Underdevelop and overexpose or underexpose and overdevelop. This is what they do."

My uncle added fuel to the fire by saying, "Not even a mount for the two rupees he charged!"

Jayraj put away the photograph and said, "Well, mounting and framing is my duty, even if you bring the photo of a donkey's rear." While he paused for breath my uncle tried to say something, but Jayraj didn't give him a chance. He said, "Here I am in the heart of the city ready to serve our townfolk. Why can't people make use of me instead of some tenth-rate camera-meddler? I am open twenty-four hours of the day in the service of humanity. I even sleep here when there is work to do, and no factory act applies to me. I can't demand overtime or bonus, but my satisfaction lies in serving humanity." He pointed at his camera, a hooded apparatus on a tripod in a corner. "There it is, always ready. If somebody summons me I respond immediately, no matter what the subject is—a wedding, a corpse, prostitute, a minister of state, or a cat on a wall—it's all the same to me. My business is to photograph, and let me tell you straight away that my charges are more than moderate. I don't believe in doing cheap work. I photographed Mahatma Gandhi when he was here. I was summoned to Madras whenever Nehru was on a visit. Dr. Radhakrishnan, Tagore, Birla, I could give you a big list of people who were pleased with my work and wrote out testimonials spontaneously. I have locked them in the safe at home. Any day you will be welcome to visit my humble home and peruse them if you like. I don't mind losing all my gold, but not the testimonials from the brilliant sons of our motherland. I want my children and their children to cherish them and say some day, "We come of a line who served the brilliant sons of Mother India, and here are the tokens."

While this preamble was going on, his hands were busy giving the finishing touches to a wedding group; he was smoothing off the ripples of glue on the back of the picture. He squatted on his heels on the floor with a little work-bench in front of him. He held the wedding group at arm's length and said, "Not my business, so many committing the folly every week, the government looking on, while people howl about the population problem, but why can't they ban all marriages for ten years?" He packed the framed picture in an old newspaper, tied a string around it, and put it away. Now my turn. He picked up my photograph, studied it again, and remarked, "Fifty heads to be compressed on a postcard. Maybe they are only little men, but still . . . Unless you look through a magnifying glass you will never know who is who." He then asked my uncle, "Will you leave the colour of the mount, frame, and style entirely to me or have you any ideas?"

My uncle was bewildered by this question and said, "I want it to look nice, that is all. I want it to look," he repeated, "particularly nice."

"I don't doubt it," said Jayraj, who never liked the other person to end a conversation. "Well, for the tone of this print there are certain shades of wooden frames and mounts suitable, and some not suitable. If you prefer something unsuitable according to me, it'll still be done. I will wrap it up, present it to you, and collect my bill; but let me assure you that my heart will not be in it. Anyway, it is up to you," he said challengingly. My uncle seemed bewildered by all this philosophy and remained silent. He looked apprehensive and wanted to know quickly the worst. The man had placed my photograph on his desk, weighting it down with a steel measuring scale. We awaited his next move. Meanwhile more people came and took their seats on the bench, like men at a dentist's parlour. Jayraj did not bother to notice his visitors, nor did he notice the crowd passing through the market gateway, shoppers, hawkers, beggars, dogs and stray cattle and coolies with baskets on their heads, all kinds of men and women, jostling, shouting, laughing, cursing, and moving as in a mass trance; they might have been able to pass in and out more easily but for Jayraj's bench sticking across the market entrance.

A very bald man came and gingerly sat down on the bench, announcing, "The trustee has sent me." It made no impression on Jayraj, who had picked up a length of framing rod and was sawing it off noisily.

My uncle asked suddenly, "When will you give it?"

Before Jayraj could muster an answer the bald man said for the fourth time, "The trustee has sent me. . . ."

Jayraj chose this moment to tell some other young man leaning on a bicycle, "Tomorrow at one o'clock." The young man jumped on his bicycle and rode away.

The bald man began again, "The trustee . . ."

Jayraj looked at my uncle and said, "It all depends when you want it."

The bald man said, "The trustee . . . is going away to Tirupathi tomorrow . . . and wants . . ."

Jayraj completed his sentence for him, "Wants me along? Tell him I have no time for a pilgrimage."

"No, no, he wants the picture."

"Where is the hurry? Let him come back from Tirupathi."

The other looked nonplussed.

Meanwhile a woman who sold betel leaves in the market came up with a basket at her hip and asked, "When should I bring the baby?"

"Whenever the midwife advises," replied Jayraj. She blushed and threw the end of her sari over her face and laughed. "Tomorrow evening at three o'clock. Dress him in his best. Put on him all the jewellery you can, and come early. If you come late the sunlight will be gone and there will be no photo. Be sure to bring two rupees with you. No credit, and then you can give me the balance when I give you the photo in a frame."

"Ah, can't you trust me so much, sir?"

"No argument, that is my system, that is all. If I want the betel leaves in your basket I pay for it at once, so also for what I do." She went away laughing, and Jayraj said, addressing no one in particular, "She has a child every ten months. Mother is constant, but not the father." His assembly laughed at this quip. "Not my business to question the parentage. I take the picture and frame it when ordered to do so and that is all."

My uncle asked all of a sudden, "Will you be able to frame and give me the photograph now?"

"No," said Jayraj promptly, "unless you expect me to stay on and work until midnight."

"Why not? You said you could."

"Yes, sir," he replied. "I said so and I will say so again, if you command me. Will you wait and take it?"

My uncle was flabbergasted. He said, "No, I cannot. I have to go to the temple," and he brooded over his inescapable routine of prayer, meditation, dinner, and sleep.

"It's five o'clock now. Your work will take two hours— the paste must dry. We must give the paste its time to dry.

But before I can take up your work, you see that man on your side, whose scalp is shining today but once upon a time who had a shock of hair like a coir doormat," and he nodded in the direction of the bald man who was still waiting for a reply for the trustee. Jayraj continued his theme of bald pate. "About ten years ago one morning I noticed when he came to frame a calendar portrait of Brahma the Creator that he was growing thin on top; fortunately for us we cannot know the top of our own heads; and I did not tell him so that he might not feel discouraged about his matrimonial future; no one can question why or wherefore of baldness; it is much like life and death. God gives us the hair and takes it away when obviously it is needed elsewhere, that is all."

Every word that Jayraj uttered pleased the bald man, who remarked at the end of it, "Don't forget that I save on hair oil!" And he bowed his head to exhibit his shining top, at which I roared with laughter, Jayraj laughed out of courtesy, and my uncle smiled patronizingly, and into this pleasant and well-softened atmosphere the bald man pushed in a word about the business which had brought him there. "The trustee . . ." he began, and Jayraj repeated, "Oh, trustee, school trustee, temple trustee, hospital trustee, let him be anything; I have no use for trustees, and so why keep harping on them?"

The bald man sprang to his feet, approached the edge of the inner sanctum, leant forward almost in supplication, and prayed, "Please, please, don't send me back empty-handed; he will be upset, thinking that I have been loafing about."

Now Jayraj looked properly concerned and said, "He would think so, would he? All right, he shall have it even if

I have to forgo sleep tonight. No more sleep, no more rest, until the trustee is pacified. That settles it." He said finally, looking at my uncle, "Yours immediately after the trustee's, even if it means all-night vigil."

My uncle repeated, "All night! I may not be able to stay long."

"You don't have to," said Jayraj. "Please be gone, sir, and that is not going to affect my programme or promise. Trust me. You are determined to hang this young person's group picture on your wall tonight, perhaps the most auspicious date in your calendar! Yes, sir. Each unto himself is my philosophy. Tonight it shall be done. I usually charge three rupees for this size, Doctor; does it seem exorbitant to you?"

I felt startled when this man again addressed my uncle as "Doctor." My uncle considered the offer and said meekly, "The print itself costs only two rupees."

"In that case I will leave it to your sense of justice. Do you assume that frame and mount are in any sense inferior to the photo?"

Everyone on the bench looked concerned and nodded appreciatively at the progress of this dialogue (like the chorus in a Greek play) and my uncle said, "All right, three." He peeped out at the municipal clock tower. "It is past five, you won't take it up before seven?"

Jayraj said, "Never before eight."

"I have to be going. How will it reach me?"

Jayraj said, "I'll knock on your door tonight and deliver it. Maybe you could leave the charges, amounting to three rupees. Don't mistake me for asking for money in advance. You see that room." He indicated an antechamber. "It is full of pictures of gods, demons, and humans, framed in glass, ordered by people who never turned up again, and in those days I never knew how to ask for payment. If a picture is not claimed immediately I keep it for twenty years in that room. That's the law here. Anyway I don't want to keep your picture for twenty years. I will bring it to you tonight . . . or . . ." A sudden idea struck him. "Why don't you leave this little fellow behind? He will collect the picture, and I will see that he comes home to you safely tonight."

An impossible idea it seemed at first. My uncle shook his head and said, "Oh, not possible. How can he stay here?"

"Trust me, have you no trust in me? Anyway at the end of the day I will deliver him and the photo at your door."

"If you are coming our way, why do you want this boy to be left here?"

"To be frank, in order to make sure that I keep my promise and don't yield to any sudden impulse to shut my shop and run home."

"Until midnight?"

"Oh, no, I was joking. Much earlier, much earlier."

"What will he do for food? He is used to his supper at eight."

Jayraj pointed to a restaurant across the street and said, "I will nourish him properly. I love to have children around."

My uncle looked at me and asked, "Will you stay?"

I was thrilled. Jayraj was going to give me heavenly things to eat, and I could watch the procession of people and vehicles on Market Road. I pleaded, "Uncle, don't be afraid." I recollected all the dare-devilry of young men in the adventure stories I had heard. I wanted to have the pride of some achievement today. I pleaded with my uncle, "Please leave me and go. I will come home later."

Jayraj looked up and said, "Don't worry about him," and held out his hand. My uncle took out his purse and counted out three rupees on Jayraj's palm saying, "I have never left him alone before."

Jayraj said, "Our boys must learn to get on by themselves. We must become a strong nation."

After my uncle left, Jayraj pushed away my photo on to the floor and took in its place on the desk a group photo of the trustee's. He kept gazing on it and said, "Not a very good photo. That Pictograph man again! So proud of his electronic flash! He claims he commands sunlight at his finger tips, but when he throws it on to the faces of a group before the camera, what do they do? They shut their eyes or open them wide as if they saw a ghost. For all the garland on his chest and all his pomposity, the man at the centre and all others in the group look to me like monkeys surprised on a mango tree. . . ." The bald head kept swaying in approval. Jayraj constantly looked up from his work to make sure that the fellow was listening. I sat between them. Jayraj abruptly ordered, "Child, move over, let that man come nearer." I obeyed instantly.

This was my first day out, exciting and frightening at the same time. The world looked entirely different—the crowd at the market, which had seemed so entertaining before, was now terrifying. I feared that I might be engulfed and swept off, and never see my home again. As twilight came on and the street lamps were lit, I grew apprehensive. Somehow I felt I could not trust Jayraj. I stole a look at him. He looked forbidding. He wore a pair of glasses with thick lenses through which his eyeballs bulged, lending him a ghoulish look; unshaven chin and grey mottled hair covering his forehead; khaki shirt and a blood-red dhoti, a frightening combination. All his smiles and friendly talk before my uncle was a show to entice me. He seemed to have his own sinister plans to deal with me once I was left at his mercy. He had become cold and aloof. Otherwise, why should he have asked me to yield my place to the bald man? The moment my uncle's back was turned this man's manner had changed; he looked grim and ignored me. Where was the nourishment he had promised? I was afraid to ask. I kept looking at the restaurant across the road in the hope that he might follow my gaze and take the hint, but his hands were sawing, hammering, pasting, and smoothing while his tongue wagged uninterruptedly. Having promised me nourishment, this man was not giving it a thought. Suppose I reminded him? But I lacked the courage to speak to him. With unappeased hunger on one side, my mind was also busy as to how to retrieve my photo from this horrible man and find my way home. I had not noticed the landmarks while coming. There were so many lanes ending on Market Road. I was not sure which one of them would lead me to Kabir Street, and from Kabir Street should I go up or down? A well stood right in the middle of that street, and beside it the striped wall of an abandoned temple in which the tailor was supposed to live. One went past it and came through onto Vinayak Street somehow. Vinayak Street seemed such a distant dream to me now. Once some gracious god could put me down there, at either end, I could always find my way home. I was beginning to feel lost.

Jayraj paused for a moment to look at me and say, "When I promise a time for delivery, I keep it." Analysing his statement, I found no hint of anything to eat. "When I promise a time . . . etc." What of the promise of food? What did "delivery" mean? Did it include eating? It was a worrying situation for me. I could not understand whether he implied that after delivering his picture to the bald man he would summon the restaurant-keeper and order a feast, or did he simply mean that in due course he would nail my photo on four sides with wood and glass and then say, "That is all, now get out." When I tried to declare, "I am very hungry, are you doing anything about it? A promise is sacred and inescapable," I found my voice croaking, creaking, and the words in such a jumble and mumble that it only attracted the other's attention and conveyed nothing. He looked up and asked, "Did you speak?"

He looked fierce under the kerosene "power-light" hanging from the ceiling, and the huge shadow of its tin reflector left half the shop in darkness. I had no doubt that he enticed people in there, murdered them in cold blood, and stored their bodies in the anteroom. I remembered his mysterious references to the room, and my uncle had understood. The wonder was that Uncle should listen to all that and yet leave me behind. Of course, if it came to it, I could hit him with the little rod on the work bench and run away. This was a testing time, and Uncle perhaps wanted to try me out; hadn't they agreed that little boys should become tough? If he asked me in I should take care not to cross the threshold—but if he ordered food, but kept it as a bait far inside and then said, "Come in here and eat"—perhaps then I should make a dash for the food, hit him with the steel rod, and run—tactics to be accomplished at lightning speed. Perhaps my uncle expected me to perform such deeds, and would admire my pluck. Hit Jayraj on the head and run and munch while running. While my mind was busy working out the details of my retreat, I noticed that the man had risen to his feet and was rummaging among old paper and cardboard, stacked in the back room. When he stood up he looked lanky and tall, with long legs and long limbs as if he had uncoiled himself. Rather snakelike, I thought.

For a moment I was seized with panic at the prospect of combating him. The bald man had edged closer and closer and had now actually stepped into the workshop, anticipating some excitement, the light from the power-lamp imparting a blinding lustre to his bald pate. Jayraj cried from the backroom, "Impossible to get at what one wants in this cursed place, must set apart a day for cleaning up. . . . Ah, here it is." And he brought out a portrait in a grey mount, took it close to the light, and said, "Come nearer, the print is rather faded." They examined it with their heads abutting each other. I looked away. I realized that while they were brewing their nefarious plan I should remain alert but without giving them any sign of noticing. "This is the man; at one time the richest doctor in Burma . . ." I caught these words. Occasionally from time to time I turned my head just to look at them and caught them glancing at me and turning away. I too looked away, sharpening my ears not to miss a single word; somehow I was beginning to feel that their talk had something to do with me. Jayraj's loud and guffawing tone was all gone, he was now talking in a sinister undertone. "Ten doctors employed under him. But this fellow was only a chokra; he sterilized needles and wrapped up powders and medicine bottles and cleansed the syringe; actually he must have started as this man's [tapping the photo] personal bootboy. When the Japanese bombed Rangoon, these people trekked back to our country, leaving behind their palatial home and several cars and everything, but still they managed to carry with them jew-ellery and much gold, and a bank account in Madras, and above all also a fifteen-day-old baby in arms. The doctor took ill and died on the way. There were rumours that he was pushed off a cliff by so-and-so. The lady reached India half dead, lingered for a year, and died. The baby was all right, so was the chokra, all through the expedition. The chokra, becoming all in all, took charge of all the cash and gold and bank accounts after reaching this country, imper-sonating the doctor. That poor woman, the doctor's wife, need not have died, but this fellow kept her a prisoner in the house and gave her some injections and finished her. The cremation was a double-quick affair across the river."

The bald man now moved back to my side. Jayraj had re-sumed his seat and was working on a frame. I still kept fixedly looking away, feeling desperate at the prospect be-fore me—a total darkness had now fallen on the city, and there was the hopelessness of getting any refreshment.

They continued their talk in conspiratorial tones all through. The bald man asked some question. Jayraj re-plied, "Who could say? I didn't know much about them. I think that the fat woman must also have been there all the time and a party to it. I learnt a lot from a servant maid who brought this picture for framing one day. I told her to call for it next day. She never came. So far no sign of anyone claiming it."

"The same fellow who sat here a little while ago!" said the bald man in astonishment.

Jayraj lowered his voice and muttered, "When I called him 'Doctor'—you must have seen his face!" and then they carried on their talk for a long while, which was all inaudi-ble to me. I kept glancing at them and feeling their eyes on me all the time. Finally the taptap of the hammer ceased and he said, "All right, this is finished. Let the glue dry a bit. Anyway it must be said to his credit: he tended the child and brought him up—only God knows the full truth." He suddenly called me, held out to me the photograph salvaged from the dark chamber, and asked, "Do you wish to take this home? I can give it to you free." And they both stared at my face and the photo while he held it out. I had a momentary curiosity to look at the face of the man who had been the subject of their talk. The photo was very faded, I could glimpse only a moustache and little else; the man was in European clothes—if what they said was true, this was my father. I looked at their faces and noticed the sneering, leering expressions on them. I flung the photo back, got up without a word, and began to run.

I raced down Market Road, not aware of the direction I was taking. I heard the man shout after me, "Come, come, I will frame yours and give it to you, and then take you home." The bald man's squeaky voice added something to support his friend, but I ran. I bumped into people coming to the market and was cursed. "Have you no eyes, these boys nowadays!" I feared Jayraj might shout, "Catch him, don't let him get away." Presently I slowed down my pace. I had no sense of direction but presently noticed Jagan's sweet-mart on my right-hand side this time and knew that I was going back the way I had come. My head was drumming with Jayraj's speech. It was agonizing to picture my uncle cheating, murdering, and lying. The references to my father and mother touched me less; they were remote, unconvincing figures.

Blundering and groping along, I reached the end of

Market Road. People looked at me curiously. I did not want to betray that this was my first outing alone, and so sauntered along, tried to look casual, whistled and hummed aloud, *"Raghupati Raghava Raja Ram."* The street lighting imperceptibly dimmed and grew sparser as I reached the foot of Lawley Statue. The Lawley Extension homes were tucked far back into their respective compounds, no way of knocking on their doors for any help; not could I approach the boys leaning on their bicycles and chatting; they were senior boys who might make fun of me or beat me. A vagrant lay stretched full length on a side away from others; he looked wild and dreadful, but he kept looking at me while others would not even notice my presence. I shrank away at the foot of this terrible statue, hoping that it would not suddenly start moving and march over me. The vagrant held out his hand and said, "Give me a coin, I will buy something to eat."

I turned my shirt pocket inside out to prove my statement, "I have no money, not a paisa, and I am also hungry."

"Go home then," he ordered.

"I want to, but where is Vinayak Street?"

It was a grave risk betraying myself in this manner; if he realized that I was a lost soul he might abduct and sell me upcountry as a slave. "I will go with you and show the way, will you tell your mother to give me a little rice for my trouble?"

Mother! Mother! My mind fell into a confusion . . . of that woman who died at Uncle's hand . . . I had all along felt my aunt was my mother. "I have only an aunt, no mother," I said.

"Aunts don't like me, and so go by yourself. Go back half the way you came, count three streets and turn on your left, if you know which is your left hand, and then turn right and you will be in Kabir Street . . ."

"Oh, I know Kabir Street, and the well," I said with relief.

"Get onto it then, and take the turning beyond the well for Vinayak Street, don't wander all over the town like this. Boys like you must stay at home and read your lessons."

"Yes, sir," I said respectfully, feeling intimidated. "Once I am back I promise to read my lessons."

The directions that he gave helped me. I came through and found myself at the disused well in Kabir Street. When I reached Vinayak Street I felt triumphant. In that feeling of relief, even Jayraj's words ceased to rankle in my mind. The dogs in our street set up a stormy reception for me. At that hour the street was deserted, and the only guardians were the mongrels that roamed up and down in packs. They barked viciously at first but soon recognized me. Escorted by the friendly dogs, wagging their tails and wetting the lampposts in their delight at meeting me, I reached my house. My uncle and aunt were on the front doorstep and flung at me a jumble of inquiries. "Your uncle wanted to start out again and look for you," my aunt said.

Uncle lifted me practically half in the air in the sheer joy of our reunion, and asked, "Where is the framer? He promised to leave you here. It is past ten o'clock now."

Before I could answer my aunt said, "I told you not to trust such persons."

"Where is your photograph?"

I had not thought of an answer for that. What could I say? I only burst into tears and wept at the memory of all the confusion in my mind. Safer to weep than to speak. If I spoke I feared I might blunder into mentioning the other photo out of the darkroom.

My aunt immediately swept me in, remarking sorrowfully, "Must be very, very hungry, poor child."

I sobbed, "He didn't give me anything to eat."

All night I lay tossing in my bed. I kicked my feet against the wall and groaned, and woke up with a start from a medley of nightmares composed of the day's experience. My uncle was snoring peacefully in his room: I could see him through the open door. I sat up and watched him. He had impersonated a doctor, but it didn't seem to be a very serious charge, as I had always thought that all doctors with their rubber tubes and medical smell were play-acting all the time. Imprisoning and poisoning my mother— Mother? My aunt was my mother as far as I could see, and she was quite alive and sound. There wasn't even a faded photo of that mother as there was of my father. The photographer had said something about money and jewellery. I was indifferent to both. My uncle gave me all the money I needed, never refusing me anything at any time. Jewellery —those glittering pieces—one had better not bother about. You could not buy candy with gold, could you? To think that the refugees from Rangoon should have carried such tinsel all the way! In my own way I was analysing and examining the charges against my uncle and found them flimsy, although the picture of him emanating out of dark whispers and furtive glances, in the background of a half-lit back room, was shocking.

I needed some clarifications very urgently. My aunt, sleeping on her mat at the edge of the open courtyard, stirred. I made sure that Uncle's snores were continuing, softly rose from my bed, and went over to her side. I sat on the edge of her mat and looked at her. She had observed my restlessness and asked, "Why haven't you slept yet?"

I whispered, "Aunt, are you awake? I want to tell you something."

She encouraged me to speak. I gave her an account of Jayraj's narrative. She merely said, "Forget it. Never mention it to your uncle."

"Why?"

"Don't ask questions. Go back to your bed and sleep."

I could do nothing more. I took the advice. The next day Jayraj managed to deliver the framed photo through someone who passed this way. My uncle examined it inch by inch by the light from the courtyard, and declared, "Wonderful, good work, worth three rupees, surely." He fumbled about with a hammer and nail looking for the right place, and hung it finally over his easy chair, right below the big portrait of his ancestor on the wall.

I acted on my aunt's advice and never asked any question. As I grew up and met more people, I heard oblique references to my uncle here and there, but I ignored whatever I heard. Only once did I try to strangle a classmate at the college hostel in Madras who had gossiped about my uncle. Stirred by such information, sometimes I thought of him as a monster and I felt like pricking and deflating him the next time I met him. But when I saw him on the railway platform, waiting to receive me, the joy in his perspiring face moved me, and I never questioned him in any manner. After seeing me through the Albert Mission High School he had maintained me at a college in Madras; he wrote a postcard at least once a week, and celebrated my arrival during a vacation with continuous feasting at home. He had probably gambled away a lot more money than he had spent on me. It didn't matter. Nothing ever mattered. He never denied me anything. Again and again I was prompted to ask the question, "What am I worth? What about my parents?" but I rigorously suppressed it. Thus I maintained the delicate fabric of our relationship till the very end of his life. After his death, I examined his records—not a shade of correspondence or account to show my connection with Burma, except the lacquered casket with a dragon on it. He had bequeathed the house and all his possessions and a small annuity in the bank to me and left my aunt in my care.

Annamalai

The mail brought me only a postcard, with the message in Tamil crammed on the back of it in minute calligraphy. I was curious about it only for a minute —the handwriting, style of address, the black ink, and above all the ceremonial flourish of the language were well known to me. I had deciphered and read out to Annamalai on an average one letter every month for a decade and a half when he was my gardener, watchman, and general custodian of me and my property at the New Extension. Now the letter began: "At the Divine Presence of my old master, do I place with hesitancy this slight epistle for consideration. It's placed at the lotus feet of the great soul who gave me food and shelter and money in my lifetime, and for whose welfare I pray to the Almighty every hour of my waking life. God bless you, sir. By your grace and the grace of gods in the firmament above, I am in excellent health and spirits, and my kith and kin, namely, my younger brother Amavasai and my daughter, son-in-law, and the two grandchildren and my sister who lives four doors from me, and my maternal uncle and his children, who tend the coconut grove, are all well. This year the gods have been kind and have sent us the rains to nourish our lands and gardens and orchards. Our tanks have been full, and we work hard. . . ." I was indeed happy to have such a good report of fertility and joy from one who had nothing but problems as far as I could remember. But my happiness was short-lived. All the rosy picture lasted about ten closely packed lines, followed by an abrupt transition. I realized all this excellence of reporting was just a formality, following a polite code of epistle-writing and not to be taken literally in part or in whole, for the letter abruptly started off in an opposite direction and tone. "My purpose in addressing your honoured self just today is to inform you that I am in sore need of money. The crops have failed this year and I am without food or money. My health is poor. I am weak, decrepit, and in bed, and need money for food and medicine. My kith and kin are not able to support me; my brother Amavasai is a godly man but he is very poor and is burdened with a family of nine children and two wives, and so I beg you to treat this letter as if it were a telegram and send me money immediately. . . ." He did not specify the amount but left it to my good sense, and whatever could be spared seemed welcome. The letter bore his name at the bottom, but I knew he could not sign; he always affixed his signature in the form of a thumb impression whenever he had to deal with any legal document. I should certainly have been glad to send a pension, not once but regularly, in return for all his years of service. But how could I be sure that he had written the letter? I knew that he could neither read nor write, and how could I make sure that the author of the letter was not his brother Amavasai, that father of nine and husband of two, who might have hit upon an excellent scheme to draw a pension in the name of a dead brother?

How could I make sure that Annamalai was still alive? His last words to me before he retired were a grand description of his own funeral, which he anticipated with considerable thrill.

I looked at the postmark to make sure that at least the card had originated correctly. But the post-office seal was just a dark smudge as usual. Even if it weren't so, even if the name of his village had been clearly set forth it would not have made any difference. I was never sure at any time of the name of his village, although as I have already said I had written the address for him scores of times in a decade and a half. He would stand behind my chair after placing the postcard to be addressed on the desk. Every time I would say, "Now recite the address properly."

"All right, sir," he would say, while I waited with the pen poised over the postcard. "My brother's name is Amavasai, and it must be given to his hand."

"That I know very well, next tell me the address precisely this time." Because I had never got it right at any time.

He said something that sounded like "Mara Konam," which always puzzled me. In Tamil it meant either "wooden angle" or "cross angle" depending on whether you stressed the first word or the second of that phonetic assemblage. With the pen ready, if I said, "Repeat it," he would help me by uttering slowly and deliberately the name— but a new one this time, sounding something like "Peramanallur."

"What is it, where is it?" I asked desperately.

"My village, sir," he replied with a glow of pride—once again leaving me to brood over a likely meaning. Making allowance for wrong utterance you could translate it as "Paerumai Nallur" meaning "town of pride and goodness" or, with a change of the stress of syllables, "town of fatness and goodness." Attempting to grope my way through all this verbal wilderness, if I said, "Repeat it," he generally came out with a brand new sound. With a touch of home-sickness in his tone and with an air of making a concession to someone lacking understanding, he would say, "Write clearly NUMTHOD POST," leaving me again to wrestle with phonetics to derive a meaning. No use, as this seemed to be an example of absolute sound with no sense, with no scope for an interpretation however differently you tried to dis-tribute the syllables and stresses or whether you attempted a translation or speculated on its meaning in Tamil, Telugu, Kannada, or any of the fourteen languages listed in the In-dian Constitution. While I sat brooding over all this ver-biage flung at me, Annamalai waited silently with an air of supreme tolerance, only suggesting gently, "Write in Eng-lish . . ."

"Why in English?"

"If it could be in Tamil I would have asked that chap who writes the card to write the address also; because it must be in English I have to trouble you"—a piece of logic that sounded intricate.

I persisted. "Why not in Tamil?"

"Letters will not reach in Tamil; what our schoolmaster has often told us. When my uncle died they wrote a letter and addressed it in Tamil to his son in Conjeevaram and the man never turned up for the funeral. We all joined and buried the uncle after waiting for two days, and the son came one year later and asked, 'Where is my father? I want to ask for money.' " And Annamalai laughed at the recollec-tion of this episode. Realizing that I had better not inquire too much, I solved the problem by writing briskly one

under another everything as I heard it. And he would con-
clusively ask before picking up the card, "Have you written
via Katpadi?"

All this business would take its own time. While the
space for address on the postcard was getting filled up I secretly fretted lest any line should be crowded out, but I always managed it somehow with the edge of my pen-point.
The whole thing took almost an hour each time, but
Annamalai never sent a card home more than once a
month. He often remarked, "No doubt, sir, that the people
at home would enjoy receiving letters, but if I wrote a card
to everyone who expected it, I would be a bankrupt. When
I become a bankrupt will there be one soul among all my
relatives who will offer a handful of rice even if I starve to
death?" And so he kept his communications within practical
limits, although they provided a vital link for him with his
village home.

"How does one get to your village?" I asked.

"Buy a railway ticket, that's how," he answered, feeling
happy that he could talk of home. "If you get into the Passenger at night paying two rupees and ten annas, you will
get to Trichy in the morning. Another train leaves Trichy
at eleven, and for seven rupees and four annas, it used to be
only five fourteen before, you can reach Villipuram. One
must be awake all night, otherwise the train will take you
on, and once they demanded two rupees extra for going further because I had slept over. I begged and pleaded and
they let me go, but I had to buy another ticket next morning to get back to Katpadi. You can sleep on the station platform until midday. The bus arrives at midday and for
twelve annas it will carry you further. After the bus you
may hire a jutka or a bullock cart for six annas and then on

foot you reach home before dark; if it gets late bandits may
waylay and beat us. Don't walk too long; if you leave in the
afternoon you may reach Marakonam before sunset. But a
card reaches there for just nine paise, isn't it wonderful?" he
asked.

Once I asked, "Why do you have the address written before the message?"

"So that I may be sure that the fellow who writes for me
does not write to his own relations on my card. Otherwise
how can I know?" This seemed to be a good way of ensuring
that the postcard was not misused. It indicated a rather
strange relationship, as he often spoke warmly of that un-
seen man who always wrote his messages on postcards, but
perhaps a few intelligent reservations in accepting a friend-
ship improve human relations. I often questioned him
about his friend.

"He has also the same name as myself," he said.

I asked, "What name?"

He bowed his head and mumbled, "My . . . my own
name . . ." Name was a matter of delicacy, something not
to be bandied about unnecessarily, a point of view which
had not occurred to me at all until one day he spoke to me
anent a signboard on the gate announcing my name. He
told me point-blank when I went down to the garden,
"Take away the name-board from that gate, if you will forgive my saying so."

"Why?"

"All sorts of people read your name aloud while passing
down the road. It is not good. Often urchins and tots just
learning to spell shout your name and run off when I try to
catch them. The other day some women also read your
name and laughed to themselves. Why should they? I do

not like it at all." What a different world was his where a
name was to be concealed rather than blazoned forth in
print, ether waves, and celluloid!

"Where should I hang that board now that I have it?"

He just said, "Why not inside the house, among the pictures in the hall?"

"People who want to find me should know where I live."

"Everyone ought to know," he said, "otherwise why
should they come so far?"

Digging the garden he was at his best. We carried on
some of our choicest dialogues when his hands were wield-
ing the pickaxe. He dug and kept digging for its own sake
all day. While at work he always tied a red bandanna over his
head, knotted above his ear in pirate fashion. Wearing a pair
of khaki shorts, his bare back roasted to an ebonite shade by
the sun, he attained a spontaneous camouflage in a background of mud and greenery; when he stood ankle-deep in
slush at the bed of a banana seedling, he was indistinguish-
able from his surroundings. On stone, slope, and pit, he
moved jauntily, with ease, but indoors he shuffled and
scratched the cement floor with his feet, his joints creaked
and rumbled as he carried himself upstairs. He never felt
easy in the presence of walls and books and papers; he
looked frightened and self-conscious, tried to mute his steps
and his voice when entering my study. He came in only
when he had a postcard to address. While I sat at my desk
he would stand behind my chair, suppressing even his
normal breath lest it should disturb my work, but he could
not help the little rumbles and sighs emanating from his
throat whenever he attempted to remain still. If I did not
notice his presence soon enough, he would look in the direction of the gate and let out a drover's cry, "Hai, hai!" at a

shattering pitch and go on to explain, "Again those cows, sir. Someday they are going to shatter the gate and swallow our lawn and flowers so laboriously tended by this old fellow. Many strangers passing our gate stop to exclaim, 'See those red flowers, how well they have come up! All of it that old fellow's work, at his age!' "

Annamalai might have other misgivings about himself, but he had had no doubt whatever of his stature as a horticulturist. A combination of circumstances helped him to cherish his notions. I did nothing to check him. My compound was a quarter acre in extent and offered him unlimited scope for experimentations. I had been living in Vinayak Street until the owner of a lorry service moved into the neighbourhood. He was a relative of the municipal chairman and so enjoyed the freedom of the city. His lorries rattled up and down all day, and at night they were parked on the roadside and hammered and drilled so as to be made ready for loading in the morning. No one else in my street seemed to notice the nuisance. No use in protesting and complaining as the relative of a municipal chairman would be beyond reproach. I decided to flee since it was impossible to read or write in that street; it dawned on me that the place was not meant for my kind any more. I began to look about. I liked the lot shown by a broker in the New Extension layout who also arranged the sale of my ancient house in Vinayak Street to the same lorry-owner. I moved off with my books and writing within six months of making up my mind. A slight upland stretching away to the mountain road; a swell of ground ahead on my left and the railway line passing through a cutting, punctuated with a red gate, was my new setting. Someone had built a small cottage with a room on top and two rooms downstairs, and it was adequate for my purpose, which was to read and write in peace.

On the day I planned to move I requested my neighbour the lorry-owner to lend me a lorry for transporting myself to my new home. He gladly gave me his lorry; the satisfaction was mutual as he could go on with all the repairs and hammerings all night without a word of protest from anyone, and I for my part should look forward to the sound of only birds and breeze in my new home. So I loaded all my books and trunks onto an open truck, with four loaders perched on them. I took my seat beside the driver and bade good-by to Vinayak Street. No one to sigh over my departure, since gradually, unnoticed, I had become the sole representative of our clan in that street, especially after the death of my uncle.

When we arrived at New Extension the loaders briskly lifted the articles off the lorry and dumped them in the hall. One of them lagged behind while the rest went back to the lorry and shouted, "Hey, Annamalai, are you coming or not?" He ignored their call, and they made the driver hoot the horn.

I said to the man, "They seem to want you. . . ."

His brief reply was, "Let them." He was trying to help me put things in order. "Do you want this to be carried upstairs?" he asked, pointing at my table. The lorry hooted outside belligerently. He was enraged at the display of bad manners, went to the doorway, looked at them, and said, waving his arms, "Be off if you want, don't stand there and make donkey noise."

"How will you come back?"

"Is that your business?" he said. "Go away if you like, don't let that donkey noise trouble this gentleman."

I was touched by his solicitude, and looked up from the books I was retrieving from the packing cases, and noticed him for the first time. He was a thick-set, heavy-jowled man with a clean-shaven head covered with a turban, a pair of khaki shorts over heavy bow legs, and long arms reaching down to his knees; he had thick fingers, a broad nose, and enormous teeth stained red with betel juice and tobacco permanently pouched in at his cheek. There was something fierce as well as soft about him at the same time.

"They seem to have left," I remarked as the sound of the lorry receded.

"Let them," he said, "I don't care."

"How will you go back?" I asked.

"Why should I?" he said. "Your things are all scattered in a jumble here, and they don't have the sense to stop and help. You may have no idea, sir, what they have become nowadays."

Thus he entered my service and stayed on. He helped me to move my trunks and books and arrange them properly. Later he followed me about faithfully when I went round to inspect the garden. Whoever had owned the house before me had not bothered about the garden. It had a kind of battlement wall to mark off the back yard, and the rest was encircled with hedges of various types. Whenever I paused to examine any plant closely, Annamalai also stood by earnestly. If I asked, "What is this?"—"This?" he said, stooping close to it, "this is a *poon chedi* (flowering plant)," and after a second look at it declared what I myself was able to observe, "Yellow flowers." I learnt in course of time that his classifications were extremely simple. If he liked a plant he called it *"poon chedi"* and allowed it to flourish. If it appeared suspicious, thorny, or awry in any manner he just declared, "This is a *poondu* (weed)," and, before I had a chance to observe, would pull it off and throw it over the wall with a curse.

"Why do you curse that poor thing?"

"It is an evil plant, sir."

"What kind of evil?"

"Oh, of several kinds. Little children who go near it will have stomach ache."

"There are no children for miles around."

"What if? It can send out its poison on the air. . . ."

A sort of basement room was available, and I asked Annamalai, "Can you live in this?"

"I can live even without this," he said, and explained, "I am not afraid of devils, spirits, or anything. I can live anywhere. Did I have a room when I lived in those forests?" He flourished his arm in some vague direction. "That lorry-keeper is a rascal, sir; please forgive my talking like this in the presence of a gentleman. He is a rascal. He carried me one day in his lorry to a forest on the hill and would never let me get away from there. He had signed a contract to collect manure from those forests, and wanted someone to stay there, dig the manure, and heap it in the lorries."

"What kind of manure?"

"Droppings of birds and dung of tigers and other wild animals and dead leaves, in deep layers everywhere, and he gave me a rupee and a half a day to stay there and dig up and load the lorry when it came. I lit a fire and boiled rice and ate it, and stayed under the trees, heaped the leaves around and lit them up to scare away the tigers roaring at night."

"Why did you choose this life just for one rupee and eight annas a day?" I asked.

He stood brooding for a few moments and replied, "I don't know. I was sitting in a train going somewhere to seek a job. I didn't have a ticket. A fellow got in and demanded, 'Where is your ticket?' I searched for it here and there and said, 'Some son of a bitch has stolen my ticket.' But he understood and said, 'We will find out who that son of a bitch is. Get off the train first.' And they took me out of the train with the bundle of clothes I carried. After the train left we were alone, and he said, 'How much have you?' I had nothing, and he asked, 'Do you want to earn one rupee and eight annas a day?' I begged him to give me work. He led me to a lorry waiting outside the railway station, handed me a spade and pickaxe, and said, 'Go on in that lorry, and the driver will tell you what to do.' The lorry put me down late next day on the mountain. All night I had to keep awake and keep a fire going, otherwise sometimes even elephants came up."

"Weren't you terrified?"

"They would run away when they saw the fire, and some-times I chanted aloud wise sayings and philosophies until they withdrew . . . leaving a lot of dung around, just what that man required . . . and he sold it to the coffee estates and made his money. . . . When I wanted to come home they would not let me, and so I stayed on. Last week when they came I was down with the shivering fever, but the lorry driver, a good man, allowed me to climb on the lorry and escape from the forest. I will never go back there, sir, that lorry man holds my wages and asserts that he has given it all as rice and potato all these months. . . . I don't know, someday you must reckon it all up for me and help me. . . ."

He left early on the following morning to fetch his baggage. He asked for an advance of five rupees, but I hesitated. I had not known him for more than twenty-four hours. I told him, "I don't have change just at this moment."

He smiled at me, showing his red-tinted teeth. "You do not trust me, I see. How can you? The world is full of rogues who will do just what you fear. You must be careful with your cash, sir. If you don't protect your cash and wife . . ." I did not hear him fully as he went downstairs muttering his comment. I was busy setting up my desk as I wished to start my work without any more delay. I heard the gate open, producing a single clear note on its hinges (which I later kept purposely on without oiling as that particular sound served as a doorbell). I peeped from my western window and saw him go down the road. I thought he was going away for good, not to return to a man who would not trust him with five rupees! I felt sorry for not giving him money, at least a rupee. I saw him go up the swell of ground and disappear down the slope. He was going by a short cut to the city across the level-crossing gate.

I went back to my desk, cursing my suspiciousness. Here was one who had volunteered to help and I had shown so little grace. That whole day he was away. Next afternoon the gate latch clicked, and the gate hummed its single clear note as it moved on its hinges, and there he was, carrying a big tin trunk on his head, and a gunny sack piled on top of it. I went down to welcome him. By the time I had gone down he had passed round the house and was lowering the trunk at the door of the basement room.

He would stand below my window and announce to the air, "Sir, I am off for a moment. I have to talk to the *mali* in the other house," and move off without waiting for my reply. Sometimes if I heard him I said, as a matter of principle, "Why do you have to go and bother him about our problems now?"

He would look crestfallen and reply, "If I must not go, I won't go, if you order so."

How could I or anyone order Annamalai? It was unthinkable, and so to evade such a drastic step I said, "You know everything, what does he know more than you?"

He would shake his head at this heresy. "Don't talk so, sir. If you don't want me to go, I won't go, that is all. You think I want to take off the time to gossip and loaf?"

A difficult question to answer, and I said, "No, no, if it is important, of course . . ."

And he moved off, muttering, "They pay him a hundred rupees a month not for nothing . . . and I want to make this compound so good that people passing should say 'Ah' when they peep through the gate . . . that is all, am I asking to be paid also a hundred rupees like that *mali?*" He moved off, talking all the way; talking was an activity performed for its own sake and needed no listener for Annamalai. An hour later he returned clutching a drooping sapling (looking more like a shot-down bird) in his hand, held it aloft under my window and said, "Only if we go and ask will people give us plants; otherwise why should they be interested?"

"What is it?" I asked dutifully, and his answer I knew even before he uttered it: "Flower plant."

Sometimes he displayed a handful of seeds tied to the end of his dhoti in a small bundle. Again I asked, "What is it?"

"Very rare seeds, no one has seen such a thing in this extension. If you think I am lying . . ." He would then ask, "Where are these to be planted?"

I would point out to a corner of the compound and say, "Don't you think we need some good covering there? All that portion looks bare. . . ." Even as I spoke I would feel the futility of my suggestion, it was just a constitutional procedure and nothing more. He might follow my instructions or his own inclination, no one could guess what he might do. He would dig up the earth earnestly at some corner and create a new bed of his own pattern, poke his forefinger into the soft earth and push the seed or the seedling in. Every morning he would stoop over it to observe minutely how it progressed. If he found a sprouting seed or any sign of life in the seedling, he watered it twice a day, but if it showed no response to his living touch, he looked outraged. "This should have come up so well, but it is the Evil Eye that scorches our plants. . . . I know what to do now." He dipped his finger in a solution of white lime and drew grotesque and strange emblems on a broken mud pot and mounted it up prominently on a stick so that those that entered our gate should first see the grotesque painting rather than the plants. He explained, "When people say, 'Ah, how good this garden looks!' they speak with envy and then it burns up the plants, but when they see the picture there, they will be filled with revulsion and our flowers will flourish. That is all."

He made his own additions to the garden each day, planting wherever he fancied, and soon I found that I could have no say in the matter. I realized that he treated me with tolerant respect rather than trust, and so I let him have his own way. Our plants grew anyhow and anywhere and generally prospered although the only attention that Annamalai gave them was an ungrudging supply of water out of a hundred-foot hose-pipe, which he turned on every leaf of every plant until it was doused and drowned. He also flung at their roots from time to time every kind of garbage and litter and called it manuring. By such assiduous efforts he created a generous, massive vegetation as a setting for my home. We had many rose plants whose nomenclature we never learnt, which had developed into leafy menacing entanglements, clawing passers-by; canna grew to gigantic heights, jasmine into wild undergrowth with the blooms maliciously out of reach although they threw their scent into the night. Dahlias pushed themselves above ground after every monsoon, presented their blooms, and wilted and disappeared, but regenerated themselves again at the next season. No one could guess who planted them originally, but nature was responsible for their periodic appearance, although Annamalai took the credit for it unreservedly. Occasionally I protested when Tacoma hedges bordering the compound developed into green ramparts, shutting off the view in every direction. Annamalai, a prince of courtesy at certain moments, would not immediately contradict me but look long and critically at the object of my protest. "Don't think of them now, I will deal with them."

"When?" I asked.

"As soon as we have the rains," he would say.

"Why should it be so late?"

"Because a plant cut in summer will die at the roots."

"You know how it is with rains these days, we never have them."

This would make him gaze skyward and remark, "How can we blame the rains when people are so evil-minded?"

"What evil?"

"Should they sell rice at one rupee a measure? Is it just? How can poor people live?"

When the rains did come eventually it would be no use reminding of his promise to trim the hedges, for he would definitely declare, "When the rain stops, of course, for if a plant is trimmed in rain, it rots. If you want the hedge to be removed completely, tell me, I will do it in a few minutes, but you must not blame me later if every passer-by in the street stares and watches the inside of the house all the time. . . ."

But suddenly one day, irrespective of his theories, he would arm himself with a scythe and hack blindly whatever came within his reach, not only the hedge I wanted trimmed but also a lot of others I preferred to keep. When I protested against this depredation, he just said, "The more we cut the better they will grow, sir." At the end of this activity, all the plants, having lost their outlines, looked battered and stood up like lean ghosts, with the ground littered green all over. At the next stage he swept up the clippings, bundled them neatly, and carried them off to his friend, namesake, and letter-writer, living in the Bamboo Bazaar, who had his cows to feed; in return for Annamalai's generosity, he kept his penmanship ever at Annamalai's service.

His gardening activities ceased late in the evening. He

laid away his implements in a corner of his basement room, laboriously coiled up the hose, and locked it away, muttering, "This is my very life; otherwise how can an old fellow feed his plants and earn a good name? If some devil steals this I am undone, and you will never see me again." So much lay behind his habit of rolling up the rubber hose, and I fancied that he slept in its coils as an added safety. After putting it away he took off his red bandanna, turned on the tap, and splashed enormous quantities of water over himself, blowing his nose, clearing his throat, and grooming himself noisily; he washed his feet, rubbing his heels on a granite slab until they shone red; now his bandanna would be employed as a towel; wiping himself dry, he disappeared into the basement and came out later wearing a shirt and a white dhoti. This was his off hour, when he visited the gate shop at the level crossing in order to replenish his stock of tobacco and gossip with friends seated on a teak log. The railway gatekeeper who owned the shop (although for reasons of policy he gave out that it belonged to his brother-in-law) was a man of information and read out a summary of the day's news to this gathering out of a local news sheet published by the man who owned the Truth Printing Press and who reduced the day's radio broadcasts and the contents of other newspapers into tiny paragraphs on a single sheet of paper, infringing every form of copyright. He brought out his edition in the evening for two paise, perhaps the cheapest newspaper in the world. Annamalai paid close attention to the reading and thus participated in contemporary history. When he returned home I could spot him half a mile away from my window as his red bandanna came into view over the crest of a slope. If he found me near at hand, he passed to me the news of the day. That was how I

first heard of John Kennedy's assassination. I had not tuned
the radio the whole day, being absorbed in some studies. I
was standing at the gate when he returned home, and I
asked casually, "What is your news today?" and he answered
without stopping, "News? I don't go hunting for it, but I
overheard that the chief ruler of America was killed today.
They said something like *Kannady* [which means glass in
Tamil]; could any man give himself such a name?"

When I realized the import of his casual reference, I said,
"Look, was it Kennedy?"

"No, they said Kannady, and someone shot him with a
gun and killed him, and probably they have already cre-
mated him." When I tried to get more news, he brushed me
off with, "Don't think I go after gossip, I only tell you what
approaches my ears . . . and they were all talking . . ."

"Who?" I asked.

"I don't know who they are. Why should I ask for names?
They all sit and talk, having nothing else to do."

He would come into my study bearing a postcard in
hand and announcing, "A letter for you. The postman
gave it." Actually it would be a letter for him, which he'd
never know until told, when he would suddenly become
tense and take a step nearer in order to absorb all the details.

"What does he say?" he would ask irritably. His only cor-
respondent was his brother Amavasai, and he hated to hear
from him. Torn between curiosity and revulsion, he would
wait for me to finish reading the postcard to myself first.
"What does that fellow have to say to me?" he would ask in
a tone of disgust and add, "as if I could not survive without such a brother!"

I'd read aloud the postcard, which always began formally with a ceremonial flourish: "To my Godly brother and protector, this insignificant younger brother Amavasai submits as follows. At this moment we are all flourishing and we also pray for our divine elder brother's welfare in one breath." All this preamble would occupy half the space on the back of the card, to be abruptly followed by mundane matters. "The boundary stone on the north side of our land was tampered with last night. We know who did it."

Pushing the tobacco on his tongue out of the way in order to speak without impediment, Annamalai would demand, "If you really know who, why don't you crack his skull? Are you bereft of all sense? Tell me that first," and glare angrily at the post card in my hand.

I'd read the following line by way of an explanation: "But they don't care."

"They don't? Why not?" The next few lines would agitate him most, but I had to read them out. "Unless you come and deal with them personally, they will never be afraid. If you keep away, nothing will improve. You are away and do not care for your kith and kin and are indifferent to our welfare or suffering. You did not care to attend even my daughter's naming ceremony. This is not how the head of a family should behave."

The rest of the letter generally turned out to be a regular charge-sheet, but concluded ceremoniously, mentioning again lotus feet and divinity. If I said, in order to divert his mind, "Your brother writes well," he would suddenly grin, very pleased at the compliment, and remark, "He to write! Oh, oh, he is a lout. That letter is written by our schoolmaster. We generally tell him our thoughts and he will write. A gifted man." He would prepare to go downstairs, remarking, "Those fellows in my village are illiterate louts. Do you think my brother could talk to a telephone?" One of his urban triumphs was that he could handle the telephone. In distinguishing the mouthpiece from the earpiece, he displayed the pride of an astronaut strolling in space. He felt an intimacy with the instrument, and whenever it rang he'd run up to announce, "Telepoon, sami," even if I happened to be near it. When I came home at night he'd always run forward to declare while opening the gate, "There was a telepoon—someone asked if you were in. . . ."

"Who was it?"

"Who? How could I know? He didn't show his face!"

"Didn't you ask his name?"

"No, what should I do with his name?"

One morning he waited at my bedroom door to tell me, "At five o'clock there was a telepoon. You were sleeping, and so I asked, 'Who are you?' He said, 'Trunk, trunk,' and I told him, 'Go away, don't trouble us. No trunk or baggage here. Master is sleeping.' " To this day I have no idea where the trunk call was from. When I tried to explain to him what a "trunk call" was (long-distance call) he kept saying, "When you are sleeping, that fellow asks for a trunk! Why should we care?" I gave up.

The only way to exist in harmony with Annamalai was to take him as he was; to improve or enlighten him would only exhaust the reformer and disrupt nature's design. At first he used to light a fire in the basement itself, his fuel consisting of leaves and all sorts of odds and ends swept up from the garden, which created an enormous pall of smoke and blackened the walls; also there was the danger of his setting fire to himself in that room without a chimney. I admonished him one day and suggested that he use charcoal. He said, "Impossible! Food cooked over charcoal shortens one's life, sir. Hereafter I will not cook inside the house at all." Next day he set up three bricks under the pomegranate tree, placed a mud pot over them, and raised a roaring fire. He boiled water and cooked rice, dhall, onion, tomato, and a variety of greens picked from the garden, and created a stew whose fragrance rose heavenward and in its passage enticed me to peep over the terrace and imbibe it.

When the monsoon set in I felt anxious as to how he was going to manage, but somehow even when the skies darkened and the rains fell, between two bouts he raised and kept up the fire under the pomegranate shade. When it poured incessantly he held a corrugated iron sheet over the fire and managed, never bothering to shield his own head. He ate at night, and preserved the remnant, and on the following day from time to time quietly dipped his fingers into the pot and ate a mouthful, facing the wall and shielding his aluminum plate from any Evil Eye that might happen to peep in at his door.

There was not a stronger person in the neighbourhood. When he stalked about during his hours of watch, tapping the ground with a metal rod and challenging in a stentorian voice, he created an air of utter intimidation, like a mastiff. God knows we might have needed a mastiff definitely in the early days, but not now. Annamalai did not seem to realize that such aggressive watch was no longer necessary. He did not seem to have noticed the transition of my surroundings from a lonely outpost (where I had often watched thieves break open a trunk and examine their booty by torchlight in a ditch a hundred yards from my bedroom window) into a populous colony, nor did he take note of the coming of the industrial estate beyond my house. If any person passing my gate dallied a minute, particularly at night after he had had his supper and the stars were out, Annamalai would challenge him to explain his presence. People passing my gate quickened their pace as a general policy. Occasionally he softened when someone asked for flowers for worship. If he saw me noticing the transaction, he would shout in rage, "Go away. What do you think you are? Do flowers come up by themselves? Here is the old fellow giving his life to tending them, and you think . . ." and charge threateningly towards the would-be worshipper; but if I remained indoors and watched through the window I could see him give a handful of flowers to the person at the gate, muting his steps and tone and glancing over his shoulder to make sure that I was not watching.

Annamalai was believed to earn money by selling my flowers, according to a lady living next door to me, who had constituted herself his implacable enemy. According to Annamalai, whenever I was away on tour she demanded of him the banana leaves grown in my garden, for her guests to dine on, and his steady refusal had angered her. Whenever I passed their compound wall she would whisper, "You are trusting that fellow too much, he is always talking to the people at the gate and always carrying on some transaction." A crisis of the first order developed once when she charged him with the theft of her fowls. She reared poultry, which often invaded my compound through a gap in the fence, and every afternoon Annamalai would be chasing them out with stones and war cries. When I was away for weeks on end, according to the lady, every other day she

missed a bird when she counted them at night. She explained how Annamalai dazed the fowl by throwing a wet
towel over its head, and carried it off to the shop at the level
crossing, where his accomplices sold or cooked it.

Once feathers were found scattered around Annamalai's
habitat when it was raided by a watchman of the municipal
sewage farm who wore a khaki coat and pretended to be a
policeman. Annamalai was duly frightened and upset. Re-
turning home from a tour one afternoon, I found Annamalai standing on a foot-high block of stone, in order to
be heard better next door, and haranguing, "You set the
police on me, do you, because you have lost a fowl? So what?
What have I to do with it? If it strays into my compound I'll
twist its neck, no doubt, but don't imagine that I will thieve
like a cheap rascal. Why go about fowl-thieving? I care two
straws for your police. They come to us for baksheesh in our
village; foolish people will not know that. I am a respectable farmer with an acre of land in the village. I grow rice.
Amavasai looks after it and writes to me. I receive letters by
post. If I am a fowl-thief, what are those that call me so?
Anyway, what do you think you are? Whom do you dare to
talk to?" In this strain he spoke for about half an hour, addressing the air and the sky, but the direction of his remarks
could not be mistaken. Every day at the same hour he delivered his harangue, soon after he had eaten his midday
food, chewed tobacco, and tied the red bandanna securely
over his ears.

Sometimes he added much autobiographical detail. Although it was beamed in the direction of the lady next door,
I gathered a great deal of information in bits and pieces
which enabled me to understand his earlier life. Mounted
on his block of stone, he said, "I was this high when I left

home. A man who has the stuff to leave home when he is only ten won't be the sort to steal fowl. My father had said, 'You are a thief. . . .' That night I slipped out of the house and walked. . . . I sat in a train going towards Madras. . . . They threw me out, but I got into the next train, and although they thrashed me and threw me out again and again, I reached Madras without a ticket. I am that kind, madam, not a fowl thief, worked as a coolie and lived in the verandahs of big buildings. I am an independent man, madam, I don't stand nonsense from others, even if it is my father. One day someone called me and put me on the deck of a steamer and sent me to a tea garden in Ceylon, where I was until the fever got me. Do you think your son will have the courage to face such things?"

At the same hour day after day I listened and could piece together his life. "When I came back home I was rid of the shivering fever. I gave my father a hundred rupees and told him that a thief would not bring him a hundred rupees. I hated my village, with all those ignorant folk. My father knew I was planning to run away once again. One day all of them held me down, decorated the house, and married me to a girl. I and Amavasai went to the fields and ploughed and weeded. My wife cooked my food. After my daughter appeared I left home and went away to Penang. I worked in the rubber estates, earned money, and sent money home. That is all they care for at home—as long as you send money they don't care where you are or what you do. All that they want is money, money. I was happy in the rubber plantations. When the Japanese came they cut off everybody's head or broke their skulls with their guns, and they made us dig pits to bury the dead and also ourselves in the end. I escaped and was taken to Madras in a boat with a lot of others. At home I found my daughter grown up, but my wife was dead. It seems she had fever every day and was dead and gone. My son-in-law is in a government job in the town. I am not a fowl thief. . . . My granddaughter goes to a school every day carrying a bag of books, with her anklets jingling and flowers in her hair. . . . I had brought the jewellery for her from Malaya." Whatever the contents of his narrative, he always concluded, "I am not a rascal. If I were a fowl thief . . . would a government officer be my son-in-law?"

I told him, "No one is listening. Why do you address the wall?"

"They are crouching behind it, not missing a word anyway," he said. "If she is a great person, let her be, what do I care? How dare she say that I stole her fowl? What do I want their fowl for? Let them keep them under their bed. I don't care. But if any creature ever strays here I'll wring its neck, that is certain."

"And what will you do with it?"

"I don't care what. Why should I watch what happens to a headless fowl?"

The postcard that most upset him was the one which said, after the usual preamble, "The black sheep has delivered a lamb, which is also black, but the shepherd is claiming it: every day he comes and creates a scene. We have locked up the lamb, but he threatens to break open the door and take away the lamb. He stands in the street and abuses us every day, and curses our family; such curses are not good for us." Annamalai interrupted the letter to demand, "Afraid of curses! Haven't you speech enough to outcurse him?" Another postcard three days later said, "They came yesterday and carried off the black sheep, the mother, when we were away in the fields."

"Oh, the . . ." He checked the unholy expression that welled up from the bottom of his heart. "I know how it must have happened. They must have kept the mother tied up in the back yard while locking up the lamb. What use would that be?" He looked at me questioningly.

I felt I must ask at this point, "Whose sheep was it?"

"The shepherd's, of course, but he borrowed ten rupees and left me the sheep as a pledge. Give me my ten rupees and take away the sheep, that is all. How can you claim the lamb? A lamb that is born under our roof is ours." This was an intricate legal point, I think the only one of its kind in the world, impossible for anyone to give a verdict on or quote precedents, as it concerned a unique kind of mortgage which multiplied in custody. "I have a set of senseless dummies managing my affairs; it is people like my brother who made me want to run away from home."

This proved a lucky break for the lady next door as the following afternoon Annamalai left to seek the company of the level-crossing gateman and other well-wishers in order to evolve a strategy to confound the erring shepherd in their village. As days passed he began to look more and more serene. I sensed that some solution had been found. He explained that someone who had arrived from the village brought the report that one night they had found the black sheep being driven off by the butcher, whereupon they waylaid him and carried it back to the bleating lamb at home. Now both the sheep and the lamb were securely locked up, while his brother and the family slept outside on the pyol of the house. I couldn't imagine how long they could continue this arrangement, but Annamalai said, "Give me back my ten rupees and take away the sheep."

"What happens to the lamb?"

"It is ours, of course. The sheep was barren until it came to our house; that shepherd boy did not pledge a pregnant sheep."

It was the tailor incident that ended our association. The postcard from home said, "The tailor has sold his machine to another tailor and has decamped. Things are bound to happen when you sit so far away from your kith and kin. You are allowing all your affairs to be spoilt." Annamalai held his temples between his hands and shut his eyes, unable to stand the shock of this revelation. I asked no questions, he said nothing more and left me, and I saw him go up the slope towards the level crossing. Later I watched him from my window as he dug at a banana root; he paused and stood frozen in a tableau with his pickaxe stuck in the ground, arms akimbo, staring at the mud at his feet. I knew at that moment that he was brooding over his domestic affairs. I went down, gently approached him, pretended to look at the banana root, but actually was dying of curiosity to know more about the tailor story. I asked some casual horticultural questions and when he started to reply I asked, "Why are tailors becoming troublesome, unpunctual, and always stealing bits of cloth?"

My antitailor sentiment softened him, and he said, "Tailor or carpenter or whoever he may be, what do I care, I am not afraid of them. I don't care for them."

"Who is the tailor your brother mentions in his letter?"

"Oh, that! A fellow called Ranga in our village, worthless fellow, got kicked out everywhere," and there the narrative for the day ended because of some interruption.

I got him to talk about the tailor a couple of days later. "People didn't like him, but he was a good tailor . . . could stitch kerchief, drawers, banian, and even women's jackets . . . but the fellow had no machine and none of his relations would help him. No one would lend him money. I got a money order from Ceylon one day for a hundred rupees—some money I had left behind. When the postman brought the money order, this tailor also came along with him, at the same moment. How could he have known? After the postman left, he asked, 'Can't you give me a hundred rupees? I can buy a machine.' I asked him, 'How did you know that I was receiving a hundred rupees, who told you?' and I slapped his face, spat at him for prying into my affairs. The fellow wept. I was, after all, his elder, and so I felt sorry and said, 'Stop that. If you howl like that I will thrash you.' Then all our village elders assembled and heard both of us, and ordered that I should lend my hundred rupees to him."

I failed to understand how anyone could order him thus. I asked naïvely, "Why should they have told you and what have they to do with it?"

He thought for a while and answered, "That is how we do it, when the elders assemble and order us . . ."

"But you didn't call the assembly?"

"I didn't, but they came and saw us, when the tailor was crying out that I had hurt him. They then wrote a bond on government paper with stamp and made him sign it; the man who sold the paper was also there, and we gave him two rupees for writing the document."

Later I got a picture of this transaction little by little. The tailor purchased a sewing machine with the loan from Annamalai. Annamalai's brother accommodated the tailor

and the machine on the pyol of his house; the tailor renewed the bond from time to time, paid the interest regularly and also a daily rent for occupying the pyol. This was a
sort of gold-edged security, and Annamalai preserved the
bond in the safety of a tin box in my cellar. When the time
for its renewal came each year, he undertook a trip to the
village and came back after a month with a fresh signature
on the bond, attested by the village headman. But now the
entire basis of their financial relationship was shaken. The
original tailor had decamped, and the new tailor did not rec-
ognize his indebtedness, although he sat on the pyol of
their house and stitched away without speaking to anyone.

"You never asked for your hundred rupees back?" I
asked.

"Why should I?" he asked, surprised at my question. "As
long as he was paying the interest, and renewing his signature. He might have been up to some mischief if I didn't
go in person; that is why I went there every time." After
all this narration, Annamalai asked, "What shall I do
now? The rascal has decamped."

"But where is the machine?"

"Still there. The new tailor stitches everybody's clothes
in our house but won't speak to us, nor does he go away
from the machine. He sleeps under it every night."

"Why don't you throw him out?"

Annamalai thought for a while and said, "He will not
speak to us and he will not pay us the rent, saying when
pressed that he paid all the rent to the first tailor along with
the price of the machine. . . . Could it be possible? Is it so
in the letter you read?"

Very soon another postcard came. It started with the re-
spected preamble, all right, but ended rather abruptly with

the words, "We have nowhere to sleep, the tailor will not move. Inside the house the sheep and the lamb are locked. As the elder of our family, tell us where we should sleep. My wives threaten to go away to their parents' houses. I am sleeping with all the children in the street. Our own house has no place for us. If you keep so far away from your kith and kin, such things are bound to happen. We suffer and you don't care."

At this point Annamalai indulged in loud thinking. "Nothing new, these women are always running off to their parents . . . if you sneeze or cough it is enough to make them threaten that they will go away. Unlucky fellow, that brother of mine. He has no guts to say, 'All right, begone, you moodhevi,' he is afraid of them."

"Why can't they throw out the tailor and lock up the machine along with the sheep? Then they could all sleep on the pyol . . ."

"I think he is the son of our wrestler—that new tailor, and you know my brother is made of straw although he has produced nine children." He considered the situation in silence for a while and said, "It is also good in a way. As long as he is not thrown out, the machine is also there. . . . God is helping us by keeping him there within our hold. If my brother has no place to sleep in, let him remain awake."

For the next three days I sensed that much confabulation was going on, as I saw the red bandanna go up the crest more often than usual. His adviser at the Bamboo Bazaar and the well-wishers at the gate shop must have attacked the core of the problem and discovered a solution. When he returned from the gate shop one evening he announced point-blank, "I must go to my village."

"Yes, why so suddenly?"

"The bond must be changed, renewed in the new tailor's name. You must let me go."

"When?"

"When? . . . Whenever you think I should go."

"I don't think you should go at all. I can't let you go now. I am planning to visit Rameswaram on a pilgrimage."

"Yes, it is a holy place, good to visit," he said patronizingly. "You will acquire a lot of merit. After you come back I will go." So we parted on the best of terms that day. As if nothing had been spoken on the subject till now, he came up again next day, stood behind my chair, and said without any preamble, "I must go."

"Yes, after I return from my pilgrimage."

He turned round and went down half way, but came up again to ask, "When are you going?"

His constant questioning put me on edge; anyway I suppressed my annoyance and replied calmly, "I am waiting for some others to join me, perhaps in ten days."

He seemed satisfied with the answer and shuffled down. That night when I returned home he met me at the gate. Hardly had I stepped in when he said, "I will be back in ten days; let me go tomorrow. I will be back in ten days and I will guard the house when you are away on pilgrimage. . . ."

"Should we settle all questions standing in the street? Can't you wait until I am in?"

He didn't answer but shut the gate and went away to his room. I felt bad all that night. While I changed my clothes, ate, and read or wrote, there was an uneasiness at the back of my mind at the memory of my sharp speech. I had sounded too severe. I went down to his back yard first thing in the morning, earlier than usual. He sat under the tap with the water turned full blast on his head, and then went dripping to his basement room. He stuck a flower on a picture of God on his wall, lit an incense stick, stuck a flower over his ear, put holy ash on his forehead, knotted the bandanna over his ear, and, dressed in his shorts, emerged ready for the day, but there was no friendliness in his eyes. I spent the time pretending to examine the mango blooms, made some appreciative remarks about the state of the garden, and suddenly said, "You want to be away for only ten days?"

"Yes, yes," he replied eagerly, his mood softening. "I must renew the bond, or gather people to throw out that interloper and seize his machine . . . even if it means bloodshed. Someone has to lose his life in this business. I will come back in ten days."

It sounded to me a too ambitious programme to be completed in ten days. "Are you sure that you want only ten days off?" I asked kindly.

"It may be a day more or less, but I promise to be back on the day I promise. Once I come back I won't go for two years, even then I won't go unless . . . I will leave the next renewal in my brother's hands."

I found myself irritated again and said, "I cannot let you go now," in a tone of extreme firmness, at which he came nearer and pleaded with his palms pressed together, "Please, I must renew the bond now; otherwise, if it is delayed, I will lose everything, and the people in my village will laugh at me."

"Get me the bond, I will have a look at it," I said with authority.

I could hear him open his black trunk. He came in bearing a swath of cloth, unwound it with tender care, and took out of its folds a document on parchment paper. I looked through it. The bond was worth a hundred rupees, and whoever had drafted it made no mention of a tailor or his machine. It was just a note promising repayment of a hundred rupees with interest from time to time, stuck with numerous stamps, dates, thumb impressions, and signatures. I really could not see how it was going to help him. I read it out to him and commented, with my fingers drumming effectively on the document, "Where is any mention of your tailor or his machine?"

"Surely there is the name Ranga on it!"

"But there is no mention of a tailor. For all it says, Ranga could be a scavenger."

Annamalai looked panic-stricken. He put his eyes close to the document and, jabbing it with his finger, asked, "What does it say here?"

I read it word by word again. He looked forlorn. I said, "I will give you a hundred rupees and don't bother about the bond. What does it cost you to reach your village?"

He made loud calculations and said, "About ten rupees by passenger from . . ."

"Coming back, ten rupees. You have been going there for years now and you have already spent more than the principal in railway fare alone to get the bond renewed."

"But he pays interest," he said.

"Give me the bond. I will pay the amount and you stay on." I felt desolate at the thought of his going away. At various times I went out on journeys short and long. Each time I just abandoned the house and returned home weeks and months later to find even a scrap of paper in the wastebasket preserved with care. Now I felt desolate.

He brushed aside my economic arguments. "You won't

know these things. I can always go to a court as long as the bond is there . . ."

"And involve yourself in further expenses? It will be cheaper to burn that bond of yours." He gave me up as a dense, impossible man whose economic notions were too elementary.

Next day and next again and again, I heard his steps on the stairs. "I will come back in ten days."

I said, "All right, all right, you have too many transactions and you have no peace of mind to do your duty here, and you don't care what happens to me. I have to change my plans for your sake, I suppose?"

All this was lost on him, it was gibberish as far as he was concerned. I was obsessed with flimsy, impalpable things while the solid, foursquare realities of the earth were really sheep and tailors and bonds. He stared at me pityingly for a moment as at an uncomprehending fool, turned, and went downstairs. The next few days I found him sulking. He answered me sharply whenever I spoke to him. He never watered the plants. He ignored the lady next door. More than all, he did not light the fire, as was his custom, in the shade of the pomegranate shrub. He had taken off the red bandanna and hooded an old blanket over his head as he sat in a corner of the basement room, in a state of mourning. When I went out or came in, he emerged from the basement and opened the gate dutifully. But no word passed between us. Once I tried to draw him into a conversation by asking breezily, "Did you hear that they are opening a new store over there?"

"I go nowhere and seek no company. Why should you think I go about, gossiping about shops and things? None of my business."

Another day I asked, "Did anyone telephone?"

"Wouldn't I mention it if there had been telepoon?" he replied, glaring at me, and withdrew mumbling, "If you have no trust in me, send me away. Why should I lie that there was no telepoon if there was one? I am not a rascal. I am also a respectable farmer; send me away." He looked like someone else under his grey hood; his angry eyes peered at me with hostility. It seemed as if he had propped himself up with an effort all these years but now was suddenly falling to pieces.

A week later one morning I heard a sound at the gate, noticed him standing outside, his tin trunk and a gunny sack stuffed with odds and ends on the ground at his feet. He wore a dark coat which he had preserved for occasions, a white dhoti, and a neat turban on his head. He was nearly unrecognizable in this garb. He said, "I am going by the eight-o'clock train today. Here is the key of the basement room." He then threw open the lid of his trunk and said, "See if I have stolen anything of yours, but that lady calls me a fowl thief. I am not a rascal."

"Why do you have to go away like this? Is this how you should leave after fifteen years of service?" I asked.

He merely said, "I am not well. I don't want to die in this house and bring it a bad name. Let me go home and die. There they will put new clothes and a fresh garland on my corpse and carry it in a procession along all the streets of our village with a band. Whereas if I am dead in that basement room while you are away, I will rot there till the municipal scavengers cart me away with the garbage heap. Let me not bring this house an evil reputation. I will go home and die. All the garden tools are in that room. Count them if you like. I am not a thief." He waited for me to inspect his trunk.

I said, "Shut it, I don't have to search your trunk." He hoisted it on his head and placed over it the gunny bundle and was starting off.

"Wait," I said.

"Why?" he asked without stopping, without turning.

"I want to give you—" I began, and dashed in to fetch some money. When I returned with ten rupees, he was gone.

A Breath of Lucifer

PROLOGUE

Nature has so designed us that we are compelled to spend at least eight hours out of twenty-four with eyes shut in sleep or in an attempt to sleep. It is a compensatory arrangement, perhaps, for the strain the visual faculty undergoes during our waking hours, owing to the glut of images impinging upon it morning till night. One who seeks serenity should, I suppose, voluntarily restrict one's range of vision. For it is mostly through the eye that the mind is strained or disturbed. Man sees more than what is necessary or good for him. If one does not control one's vision, nature will do it for one sooner or later.

Unnoticed, little by little, my right eye had been growing dimmer in the course of a year or two. I felt annoyed by the presence of a smudge of oil on the lens of my spectacles, which I pulled out and wiped with a handkerchief every other minute. When I tried to read, the smudge appeared on the first line and travelled down line by line, and it also touched up the faces of friends and foes alike whenever I happened to examine a photograph. As I raised my eyes the blot also lifted itself upward. It grew in circumference. I couldn't watch a movie without noticing an unseemly mole on the star's much prized face. No amount of cleaning of my spectacle lens was any use.

My eye doctor, after a dark-room test, pronounced that the spot was not on my spectacle lens but in the God-given lens of the eye itself, which was losing its transparency. He recorded it for my comfort on a piece of paper as "Lentil Opacity," to be remedied by means of a simple operation in due course.

Everyone speaks of the simplicity of the operation. It's simple in the sense that it is painless, accomplished without bloodshed. But to the surgeon it is a delicate and responsible task, demanding the utmost concentration of his powers at his finger tips, which will have to hover with the lightness of a butterfly over the patient's eye while detaching a tiny opalescent piece from its surface.

After the operation, total immobility in a state of total blackout for nearly a week, with both eyes sealed up with a bandage; not even the faintest ray of light may pass this barrier. The visual world is shut off. At first I dreaded the prospect. It seemed an inhuman condition of existence. But actually it turned out to be a novel experience. To observe nothing. To be oblivious of the traffic beneath my window, and of the variety of noise-makers passing up and down. I only hear the sound of the traffic but feel no irritation. Perhaps such irritations are caused as much by the sight of the irritant as by its decibel value. When you have no chance of observing the traffic, you cease to bother about it. A soundproof room may not be the only way to attain tranquillity—a bandage over one's eyes may achieve the same result. I never notice the weather, another source of despair, dismay, disappointment, or ecstasy for everyone at all times. I never know whether it is cloudy or sunny outside my window; when it rains I relish the patter of raindrops and the coolness without being aware of the slush and mess of a rain-sodden landscape. I am blissfully free alike from elation as from fury or despair. The joy stimulated by one experience could be as fatiguing as the despair caused by another. I hear words and accept them without any reservation as I am unaware of the accompanying facial expression or gesture which normally modulates the spoken word. In this state, in which one accepts the word absolutely, human relationships become suddenly simplified. For this same reason, I think, the yogis of yore advocated as a first step (and a final step also) in any technique of self-development the unwavering concentration of one's eyes on the tip of one's nose. Mahatma Gandhi himself advised a youth whose heart was constantly agitated by the sight of women to walk with his eyes fixed on his toe, or on the stars above.

When the outside world is screened off thus, one's vision turns immediately inward. In the depths of one's being (according to the terms of philosophers and mystics) or in the folds of one's brain (according to physiologists or psychologists) there is a memory-spot for every faculty. "Music when soft voices die, vibrates in the memory," said Shelley. One can recollect the fragrance of a bygone flower or a perfume, the softness of a touch. Similarly there is a visual memory too, which revives in all its sharpness under some extraordinary stimulus. The visual memory brings forth not only something seen and cherished but also wished for. My interests, let me confess, broadly speaking, are archaeological and geological. All my life I have been excessively fond of rocks, monuments, and ancient sculptures. I can never pass by a rock formation indifferently, nor an old temple or a monument. So I now watch through my bandaged eyes night and day breath-taking friezes, cornices, pillars, and carvings, countless numbers of them, as on a slow moving platform, as if one were present at the stone-cluttered yard of a super-human sculptor. Sometimes I see a goddess enthroned on a lotus seat in a corner, and not far from her is a formless slab smoothed out by time, but faint etchings, possibly edicts of some ancient emperor, are still visible on it. A closer scrutiny reveals that this whole setting is not actually a corner—there is no corner, no direction, east, west, south, or north; it is a spot without our familiar spatial relationships.

Strangely, my visual memory does not present to me any white walls or bright ceilings. Every surface is grey and ancient, as if centuries of the burning of lamps have left congealed layers of holy oil on every surface. Sometimes I am enmeshed in a jumble of chariot wheels, crowns without heads, maces, and fragments of a dilapidated throne; suddenly this jumble sorts itself out and forms into a single regal figure standing on its feet, spanning the ground and the sky. Presently all this melts out of view. The floor is strewn with sawn-off timber, and a lot of grim metallic artifacts, perhaps the leftovers of an ancient torture chamber. A fantastic contrast occurs presently—an endless billowing stretch of tarpaulin or canvas envelops the whole landscape, such enormous billows that I wonder how I can take a step forward without getting enmeshed in them. Now I find myself in a corridor of an ageless cave-temple. Although I am supposed to remain in the dark I find a subdued, serene light illuminating every object and corner softly for me, a light that throws no shadow. Nothing looks fearsome or unpleasant. Everything is in harmony with everything else and has a pleasant quality all its own. Even an occasional specimen of fauna, a tiger in shape but with the face of an angel—it is not clear what creature is represented—smoothly glides past me, throwing a friendly smile at me.

Reality is of the moment and where we are. The immediate present possesses a convincing solid quality; all else is mere recollection or anticipation. This room with the bed on which I lie day and night is very real to me, with all the spectacle that passes before me; other things seem remote and dreamlike. The present rhythm of my life is set by a routine from morning at six (as I guess from the hawkers' voices in the street), when I summon my attendant,* till the night, when I am put to bed with the announcement by the same attendant, "Light is shut off, sir," punctuated by the arrivals and departures of the doctors' team and visitors who bring me news of the unreal world in which they live. Within the confines of this existence I feel snug and contented. Its routines are of the utmost importance to me. I am so much at home within it that I suspect I shall feel a regret when it ends.

R. K. Narayan
March 1969

* Whose company and conversation have inspired me to write the accompanying story.

Sam was only a voice to me, a rich, reverberating baritone. His whispers themselves possessed a solid, rumbling quality. I often speculated, judging from his voice, what he might look like: the possessor of such a voice could be statuesque, with curls falling on his nape, Roman nose, long legs able to cover the distance from my bed to the bathroom in three strides although to me it seemed an endless journey. I asked him on the very first day, "What do you look like?"

"How can I say? Several years since I looked at a mirror!"

"Why so?"

"The women at home do not give us a chance, that is all. I have even to shave without a mirror." He added, "Except once when I came up against a large looking glass at a tailor's and cried out absent-mindedly, 'Ah, Errol Flynn in town!'"

"You admired Errol Flynn?"

"Who wouldn't? As Robin Hood, unforgettable; I saw the picture fifty times."

"What do you look like?"

He paused and answered, "Next week this time you

will see for yourself; be patient till the bandages are taken off. . . ."

Sam had taken charge of my bodily self the moment I was wheeled out of the operation theatre at the Malgudi Eye Clinic in New Extension with my eyes padded, bandaged, and sealed. I was to remain blindfolded for nearly a week in bed. During this confinement Sam was engaged for eight rupees a day to act as my eyes.

He was supposed to be a trained "male nurse," a term which he abhorred, convinced that nursing was a man's job and that the female in the profession was an impostor. He assumed a defiant and challenging pose whenever the sister at the nursing home came into my room. When she left he always had a remark to make, "Let this lady take charge of a skull-injury case; I will bet the patient will never see his home again."

Sam had not started life as a male nurse, if one might judge from his references. He constantly alluded to military matters, commands, campaigns, fatigue duties, and parades. What he actually did in the army was never clear to me. Perhaps if I could have watched his facial expressions and gestures I might have understood or interpreted his words differently, but in my unseeing state I had to accept literally whatever I heard. He often spoke of a colonel who had discovered his talent and encouraged and trained him in nursing. That happened somewhere on the Burma border, Indo-china, or somewhere, when their company was cut off and the medical units completely destroyed. The colonel had to manage with a small band of survivors, the most active among them being Sam, who repaired and rehabilitated the wounded and helped them return home almost intact when the war ended. Which war was it? Where was it fought? Against whom? I could never get an answer to those questions. He always spoke of "the enemy," but I never understood who it was since Sam's fluency could not be interrupted for a clarification. I had to accept what I heard without question. Before they parted, the colonel composed a certificate which helped Sam in his career. "I have framed it and hung it in my house beside Jesus," he said.

At various theatres of war (again, which war I could never know) his services were in demand, mainly in surgical cases. Sam was not much interested in the physician's job. He had mostly been a surgeon's man. He only spoke of incidents where he had to hold up the guts of someone until the surgeon arrived, of necks half severed, arms amputated, and all aspects of human disjointedness and pain handled without hesitancy or failure. He asserted, "My two hands and ten fingers are at the disposal of anyone who needs them in war or peace."

"What do you earn out of such service?" I asked.

He replied, "Sometimes ten rupees a day, five, two, or nothing. I have eight children, my wife, and two sisters and a niece depending on me, and all of them have to be fed, clothed, sent to schools, and provided with books and medicines. We somehow carry on. God gives me enough. The greater thing for me is the relief that I am able to give anyone in pain. . . . Oh, no, do not get up so fast. Not good for you. Don't try to swat that mosquito buzzing at your ear. You may jam your eye. I am here to deal with that mosquito. Hands down, don't put up your hand near your eyes." He constantly admonished me, ever anxious lest I should by some careless act suffer a setback.

He slept in my room, on a mat a few feet away from my

bed. He said that he woke up at five in the morning, but it could be any time since I had no means of verifying his claim by a watch or by observing the light on the walls. Night and day and all days of the week were the same to me. Sam explained that although he woke up early he lay still, without making the slightest noise, until I stirred in bed and called, "Sam!"

"Good morning, sir," he answered with alacrity and added, "Do not try to get up yet." Presently he came over and tucked up the mosquito net with scrupulous care. "Don't get up yet," he ordered and moved off. I could hear him open the bathroom door. Then I noticed his steps move farther off as he went in to make sure that the window shutters were secure and would not fly open and hit me in the face when I got in and fumbled about. After clearing all possible impediments in my way, he came back and said, "Righto, sir, now that place is yours, you may go in safely. Get up slowly. Where is the hurry? Now edge out of your bed, the floor is only four inches below your feet. Slide down gently, hold my hand, here it is. . . ." Holding both my hands in his, he walked backward and led me triumphantly to the bathroom, remarking along the way, "The ground is level and plain, walk fearlessly . . ."

With all the assurance that he attempted to give me, the covering over my eyes subjected me to strange tricks of vision and made me nervous at every step. I had a feeling of passing through geological formations, chasms, and canyons or billowing mounds of cotton wool, tarpaulin, or heaps of smithy junk or an endless array of baffle walls one beside another. I had to move with caution. When we reached the threshold of the bathroom he gave me precise directions: "Now move up a little to your left. Raise your right foot, and there you are. Now you do anything here. Only don't step back. Turn on your heel, if you must. That will be fine." Presently, when I called, he re-entered the bathroom with a ready compliment on his lips: "Ah, how careful and clean! I wish some people supposed to be endowed with full vision could leave a W.C. as tidy! Often, after they have been in, the place will be fit to be burnt down! However, my business in life is not to complain but to serve." He then propelled me to the washbasin and handed me the toothbrush. "Do not brush so fast. May not be good for your eyes. Now stop. I will wash the brush. Here is the water for rinsing. Ready to go back?"

"Yes, Sam!"

He turned me round and led me back towards my bed. "You want to sit on your bed or in the chair?" he asked at the end of our expedition. While I took time to decide, he suggested, "Why not the chair? You have been in bed all night. Sometimes I had to mind the casualties until the stretcher-bearers arrived, and I always said to the boys, 'Lying in bed makes a man sick, sit up, sit up as long as you can hold yourselves together.' While we had no sofas in the jungle, I made them sit and feel comfortable on anything, even on a snake-hole once, after flattening the top."

"Where did it happen? Did you say Burma?" I asked as he guided me to the cane chair beside the window.

He at once became cautious. "Burma? Did I say Burma? If I mentioned Burma I must have meant it and not the desert—"

"Which campaign was it?"

"Campaign? Oh, so many, I may not remember. Anyway it was a campaign and we were there. Suppose I fetch you my diary tomorrow? You can look through it when your eyes are all right again, and you will find in it all the answers.

"Oh! that will be very nice indeed."

"The colonel gave me such a fat, leather-bound diary, which cost him a hundred rupees in England, before he left, saying, 'Sam, put your thoughts into it and all that you see and do, and some day your children will read the pages and feel proud of you.' How could I tell the colonel that I could not write or read too well? My father stopped my education when I was that high, and he devoted more time to teach me how to know good toddy from bad."

"Oh, you drink?" I asked.

"Not now. The colonel whipped me once when he saw me drunk, and I vowed I'd never touch it again," he added as an afterthought while he poured coffee for me from the Thermos flask (which he filled by dashing out to a coffee house in the neighborhood; it was amazing with what speed he executed these exits and entrances, although to reach the coffee house he had to run down a flight of steps, past a verandah on the ground floor, through a gate beyond a drive, and down the street; I didn't understand how he managed it all as he was always present when I called him, and had my coffee ready when I wanted it). He handed me the cup with great care, guiding my fingers around the handle with precision. While I sipped the coffee I could hear him move around the bed, tidying it up. "When the doctor comes he must find everything neat. Otherwise he will think that a donkey has been in attendance in this ward." He swept and dusted. He took away the coffee cup, washed it at the sink and put it away, and kept the toilet flush hissing and roaring by repeated pulling of the chain. Thus he set the stage for the doctor's arrival. When the sound of the wheels of the bandage-trolley was heard far off, he helped me back to my bed and stationed himself at the door. When footsteps approached, the baritone greeted: "Good morning, Doctor sir."

The doctor asked, "How is he today?"

"Slept well. Relished his food. No temperature. Conditions normal, Doctor sir." I felt the doctor's touch on my brow as he untied the bandage, affording me for a tenth of a second a blurred view of assorted faces over me; he examined my eye, applied drops, bandaged again, and left. Sam followed him out as an act of courtesy and came back to say, "Doctor is satisfied with your progress. I am happy it is so."

Occasionally I thumbed a little transistor radio, hoping for some music, but turned it off the moment a certain shrill voice came on the air rendering "film hits"; but I always found the tune continuing in a sort of hum for a minute or two after the radio was put away. Unable to judge the direction of the voice or its source, I used to feel puzzled at first. When I understood, I asked, "Sam, do you sing?"

The humming ceased. "I lost practice long ago," he said, and added, "When I was at Don Bosco's, the bishop used to encourage me. I sang in the church choir, and also played the harmonium at concerts. We had our dramatic troupe too and I played Lucifer. With my eyebrows painted and turned up, and with a fork at my tail, the bishop often said that never a better Lucifer was seen anywhere; and the public appreciated my performance. In our story the king was a good man, but I had to get inside him and poison his nature. The princess was also pure but I had to spoil her heart and make her commit sins." He chuckled at the memory of those days.

He disliked the nurse who came on alternate days to give

me a sponge bath. Sam never approved of the idea. He said,
"Why can't I do it? I have bathed typhoid patients running
one hundred and seven degrees—"

"Oh, yes, of course." I had to pacify him. "But this is different, a very special training is necessary for handling an
eye patient."

When the nurse arrived with hot water and towels he
would linger on until she said unceremoniously, "Out you
go, I am in a hurry." He left reluctantly. She bolted the
door, seated me in a chair, helped me off with my clothes,
and ran a steaming towel over my body, talking all the time
of herself, her ambition in life to visit her brother in East
Africa, of her three children in school, and so forth.

When she left I asked Sam, "What does she look like?"

"Looks like herself all right. Why do you want to bother
about her? Leave her alone. I know her kind very well."

"Is she pretty?" I asked persistently, and added, "At any
rate I can swear that her voice is sweet and her touch
silken."

"Oh! Oh!" he cried. "Take care!"

"Even the faint garlic flavour in her breath is very pleas-
sant, although normally I hate garlic."

"These are not women you should encourage," he said.
"Before you know where you are, things will have happened. When I played Lucifer, Marie, who took the part of
the king's daughter, made constant attempts to entice me
whenever she got a chance. I resisted her stoutly, of course;
but once when our troupe was camping out, I found that
she had crept into my bed at night. I tried to push her off,
but she whispered a threat that she would yell at the top of
her voice that I had abducted her. What could I do with
such a one!" There was a pause, and he added, "Even after

we returned home from the camp she pursued me, until one day my wife saw what was happening and gashed her face with her fingernails. That taught the slut a lesson."

"Where is Marie these days?" I asked.

He said, "Oh! she is married to a fellow who sells raffle tickets, but I ignore her whenever I see her at the market gate helping her husband."

When the sound of my car was heard outside, he ran to the window to announce, "Yes sir, they have come." This would be the evening visit from my family, who brought me my supper. Sam would cry from the window, "Your brother is there and that good lady his wife also. Your daughter is there and her little son. Oh! what a genius he is going to be! I can see it in him now. Yes, yes, they will be here in a minute now. Let me keep the door open." He arranged the chairs. Voices outside my door, Sam's voice overwhelming the rest with "Good evening, madame. Good evening, sir. Oh! You little man! Come to see your grandfather! Come, come nearer and say hello to him. You must not shy away from him." Addressing me, he would say, "He is terrified of your beard, sir," and, turning back to the boy, "He will be all right when the bandage is taken off. Then he is going to have a shave and a nice bath, not the sponge bath he is now having, and then you will see how grand your grandfather can be!" He then gave the visitors an up-to-the-minute account of the state of my recovery. He would also throw in a faint complaint. "He is not very cooperative. Lifts his hands to his eyes constantly, and will not listen to my advice not to exert." His listeners would comment on this, which would provoke a further comment in the great baritone, the babble maddening to one not able to watch faces and sort out the speakers, until I implored, "Sam, you can retire for a while and leave us. I will call you later"— thus giving me a chance to have a word with my visitors. I had to assume that he took my advice and departed. At least I did not hear him again until they were ready to leave, when he said, "Please do not fail to bring the washed clothes tomorrow. Also, the doctor has asked him to eat fruits. If you could find apples—" He carried to the car the vessels brought by them and saw them off.

After their departure he would come and say, "Your brother, sir, looks a mighty officer. No one can fool him, very strict he must be, and I dare not talk to him. Your daughter is devoted to you, no wonder, if she was mother-less and brought up by you. That grandson! Watch my words, some day he is going to be like Nehru. He has that bearing now. Do you know what he said when I took him out for a walk? 'If my grandfather does not get well soon I will shoot you.' " And he laughed at the memory of that pugnacious remark.

We anticipated with the greatest thrill the day on which the bandages would be taken off my eyes. On the eve of the memorable day Sam said, "If you don't mind, I will arrange a small celebration. This is very much like the New Year Eve. You must sanction a small budget for the ceremony, about ten rupees will do. With your permission—" He put his hand in and extracted the purse from under my pillow. He asked for an hour off and left. When he returned I heard him place bottles on the table.

"What have you there?" I asked.

"Soft drinks, orange, Coca-Cola, this also happens to be my birthday. I have bought cake and candles, my humble contribution for this grand evening." He was silent and busy for a while and then began a running commentary: "I'm now cutting the cake, blowing out the candles—"

"How many?"

"I couldn't get more than a dozen, the nearby shop did not have more."

"Are you only twelve years old?"

He laughed, handed me a glass. "Coca-Cola, to your health. May you open your eyes on a happy bright world—"

"And also on your face!" I said. He kept filling my glass and toasting to the health of all humanity. I could hear him gulp down his drink again and again. "What are you drinking?"

"Orange or Coca-Cola, of course."

"What is the smell?"

"Oh, that smell! Someone broke the spirit lamp in the next ward."

"I heard them leave this evening!"

"Yes, yes, but just before they left they broke the lamp. I assured them, 'Don't worry, I'll clean up.' That's the smell on my hands. After all, we must help each other—" Presently he distributed the cake and burst into a song or two: "*He's a jolly good fellow*," and then, "*The more we are together—*" in a stentorian voice. I could also hear his feet tapping away a dance.

After a while I felt tired and said, "Sam, give me supper. I feel sleepy."

After the first spell of sleep I awoke in the middle of the night and called, "Sam."

"Yes, sir," he said with alacrity.

"Will you lead me to the bathroom?"

"Yes, sir." The next moment he was at my bed, saying,

"Sit up, edge forward, two inches down to your feet; now left, right, left, march, left, right, right turn." Normally, whenever I described the fantastic things that floated before my bandaged eyes he would reply, "No, no, no wall, nor a pillar. No junk either, trust me and walk on—" But today when I said, "You know why I have to walk so slowly?"—

"I know, I know," he said. "I won't blame you. The place is cluttered."

"I see an immense pillar in my way," I said.

"With carvings," he added. "Those lovers again. These two figures! I see them. She is pouting her lips, and he is trying to chew them off, with his arm under her thigh. A sinful spectacle, that's why I gave up looking at sculptures!"

I tried to laugh it off and said, "The bathroom."

"The bathroom, the bathroom, that is the problem. . . ." He paused and then said all of a sudden, "The place is on fire."

"What do you mean on fire?"

"I know my fire when I see one. I was Lucifer once. When I came on stage with fire in my nostrils, children screamed in the auditorium and women fainted. Lucifer has been breathing around. Let us go." He took me by my hand and hurried me out in some direction.

At the verandah I felt the cold air of the night in my face and asked, "Are we going out—?"

He would not let me finish my sentence. "This is no place for us. Hurry up. I have a responsibility. I cannot let you perish in the fire."

This was the first time I had taken a step outside the bedroom, and I really felt frightened and cried, "Oh! I feel we are on the edge of a chasm or a cavern, I can't walk." And he

said, "Softly, softly. Do not make all that noise. I see the
tiger's tail sticking out of the cave."

"Are you joking?"

He didn't answer but gripped my shoulder and led me
on. I did not know where we were going. At the stairhead he
commanded, "Halt, we are descending, now your right foot
down, there, there, good, now bring the left one, only
twenty steps to go." When I had managed it without stum-
bling, he complimented me on my smartness.

Now a cold wind blew in my face, and I shivered. I asked,
"Are we inside or outside?" I heard the rustle of tree leaves.
I felt the gravel under my bare feet. He did not bother to
answer my question. I was taken through a maze of garden
paths, and steps. I felt bewildered and exhausted. I suddenly stopped dead in my tracks and demanded, "Where are
you taking me?" Again he did not answer. I said, "Had we
better not go back to my bed?"

He remained silent for a while to consider my proposal
and agreed, "That might be a good idea, but dangerous.
They have mined the whole area. Don't touch anything you
see, stay here, don't move, I will be back." He moved off. I
was seized with panic when I heard his voice recede. I heard
him sing *"He's a jolly good fellow, He's a jolly good fellow,"*
followed by *"Has she got lovely cheeks? Yes, she has lovely
cheeks,"* which was reassuring as it meant that he was still
somewhere around.

I called out, "Sam."

He answered from afar, "Coming, but don't get up yet."

"Sam, Sam," I pleaded, "let me get back to my bed. Is it
really on fire?"

He answered, "Oh, no, who has been putting ideas into
your head? I will take you back to your bed, but please give

me time to find the way back. There has been foul play and our retreat is cut off, but please stay still and no one will spot you." His voice still sounded far off.

I pleaded desperately, "Come nearer." I had a feeling of being poised over a void. I heard his approaching steps.

"Yes, sir, what is your command?"

"Why have you brought me here?" I asked.

He whispered, "Marie, she had promised to come, should be here any minute." He suddenly cried out, "Marie, where are you?" and mumbled, "She came into your room last night and the night before, almost every night. Did she disturb you? No. She is such a quiet sort, you would never have known. She came in when I put out the light, and left at sunrise. You are a good officer, have her if you like."

I could not help remarking, "Didn't your wife drive her away?"

Promptly came his reply: "None of her business. How dare she interfere in my affairs? If she tries . . ." He could not complete the sentence, the thought of his wife having infuriated him. He said, "That woman is no good. All my troubles are due to her."

I pleaded, "Sam, take me to my bed."

"Yes, sir," he said with alacrity, took my hand, and led me a few steps and said, "Here is your bed," and gave me a gentle push down until I sank at my knee and sat on the ground. The stones pricked me, but that seemed better than standing on my feet. He said, "Well, blanket at your feet. Call out 'Sam,' I am really not far, not really sleeping. . . . Good night, good night, I generally pray and then sleep, no, I won't really sleep. 'Sam,' one word will do, one word will do . . . will do. . . ." I heard him snore, he was sound asleep somewhere in the enormous void. I resigned myself to my fate. I put out my hand and realized that I was beside a bush, and I only hoped that some poisonous insect would not sting me. I was seized with all sorts of fears.

The night was spent thus. I must have fallen into a drowse, awakened at dawn by the bird-noises around. A woman took my hand and said, "Why are you here?"

"Marie?" I asked.

"No, I sweep and clean your room every morning, before the others come."

I only said, "Lead me to my bed."

She did not waste time on questions. After an endless journey she said, "Here is your bed, sir, lie down."

I suffered a setback, and the unbandaging was postponed. The doctor struggled and helped me out of a variety of ailments produced by shock and exposure. A fortnight later the bandages were taken off, but I never saw Sam again. Only a postcard addressed to the clinic several days later:

"I wish you a speedy recovery. I do not know what happened that night. Some foul play, somewhere. That rogue who brought me the Coca-Cola must have drugged the drink. I will deal with him yet. I pray that you get well. After you go home, if you please, send me a money order for Rs. 48/—. I am charging you for only six days and not for the last day. I wish I could meet you, but my colonel has summoned me to Madras to attend on a leg amputation. . . . Sam."

Seventh House

Krishna ran his finger over the block of ice in order to wipe away the layer of sawdust, chiselled off a piece, crushed it, and filled the rubber ice bag. This activity in the shaded corner of the back verandah gave him an excuse to get away from the sickroom, but he could not dawdle over it, for he had to keep the icecap on his wife's brow continuously, according to the doctor's command. In that battle between ice and mercury column, it was ice that lost its iciness while the mercury column held its ground at a hundred and three degrees Fahrenheit. The doctor had looked triumphant on the day he diagnosed the illness as typhoid, and announced with glee, "We now know what stick to employ for beating it; they call it Chloromycetin. Don't you worry any more." He was a good doctor but given to lugubrious humour and monologuing.

The Chloromycetin pills were given to the patient as directed, and at the doctor's next visit Krishna waited for him to pause for breath and then cut in with "The fever has not gone down," holding up the temperature chart.

The doctor threw a brief, detached look at the sheet and continued, "The municipality served me a notice to put a slab over the storm drain at my gate, but my lawyer said—"

"Last night she refused food," Krishna said.

"Good for the country, with its food shortage. Do you know what the fat grain merchant in the market did? When he came to show me his throat, he asked if I was an M.D.! I don't know where he learned about M.D.s."

"She was restless and tugged at her bedclothes," Krishna said, lowering his voice as he noticed his wife open her eyes.

The doctor touched her pulse with the tip of his finger and said breezily, "Perhaps she wants a different-coloured sheet, and why not?"

"I have read somewhere the tugging of bedclothes is a bad sign."

"Oh, you and your reading!"

The patient moved her lips. Krishna bent close to her, and straightened himself to explain, "She is asking when you will let her get up."

The doctor said, "In time for the Olympics . . ." and laughed at his own joke. "I'd love to be off for the Olympics myself."

Krishna said, "The temperature was a hundred and three at one a.m. . . ."

"Didn't you keep the ice going?"

"Till my fingers were numb."

"We will treat you for cramps by and by, but first let us see the lady of the house back in the kitchen."

So Krishna found, after all, a point of agreement with the doctor. He wanted his wife back in the kitchen very badly. He miscooked the rice in a different way each day, and swallowed it with buttermilk at mealtimes and ran back to his wife's bedside.

The servant maid came in the afternoon to tidy up the

patient and the bed, and relieved Krishna for almost an hour, which he spent in watching the street from the doorway: a cyclist passing, schoolchildren running home, crows perching in a row on the opposite roof, a street hawker crying his wares—anything seemed interesting enough to take his mind off the fever.

Another week passed. Sitting there beside her bed, holding the ice bag in position, he brooded over his married life from its beginning.

When he was studying at Albert Mission he used to see a great deal of her; they cut their classes, sat on the river's edge, discussed earnestly their present and future, and finally decided to marry. The parents on both sides felt that here was an instance of the evils of modern education: young people would not wait for their elders to arrange their marriage but settled things for themselves, aping Western manners and cinema stories. Except for the lack of propriety, in all other respects the proposal should have proved acceptable; financial background of the families, the caste and group requirements, age, and everything else were correct. The elders relented eventually, and on a fine day the horoscopes of the boy and girl were exchanged and found not suited to each other. The boy's horoscope indicated Mars in the Seventh House, which spelled disaster for his bride. The girl's father refused to consider the proposal further. The boy's parents were outraged at the attitude of the bride's party—a bride's father was a seeker and the bridegroom's the giver, and how dare they be finicky? "Our son will get a bride a hundred times superior to this girl. After all, what has she to commend her? All college girls make themselves up to look pretty, but that is not everything." The young couple felt and looked miserable, which induced the parents to reopen negotiations. A wise man suggested that, if other things were all right, they could ask for a sign and go ahead. The parties agreed to a flower test. On an auspicious day they assembled in the temple. The wick lamp in the inner sanctum threw a soft illumination around. The priest lit a piece of camphor and circled it in front of the image in the sanctum. Both sets of parents and their supporters, standing respectfully in the pillared hall, watched the image and prayed for guidance. The priest beckoned to a boy of four who was with another group of worshippers. When he hesitated, the priest dangled a piece of coconut. The child approached the threshold of the sanctum greedily. The priest picked off a red and a white flower from the garland on the image, placed them on a tray, and told the boy to choose one.

"Why?" asked the boy, uneasy at being watched by so many people. If the red flower was chosen, it would indicate God's approval. The little boy accepted the piece of coconut and tried to escape, but the priest held him by the shoulder and commanded, "Take a flower!" at which the child burst into tears and wailed for his mother. The adults despaired. The crying of the child at this point was inauspicious; there should have been laughter and the red flower. The priest said, "No need to wait for any other sign. The child has shown us the way," and they all dispersed silently.

Despite the astrologers, Krishna married the girl, and Mars in the Seventh House was, eventually, forgotten.

The patient seemed to be asleep. Krishna tiptoed out of the room and told the servant maid waiting in the verandah, "I have to go out and buy medicines. Give her orange juice at six, and look after her until I return." He stepped out of his house, feeling like a released prisoner. He walked along, enjoying the crowd and bustle of Market Road until the thought of his wife's fever came back to his mind. He desperately needed someone who could tell him the unvarnished truth about his wife's condition. The doctor touched upon all subjects except that. When Chloromycetin failed to bring down the fever, he said cheerfully, "It only shows that it is not typhoid but something else. We will do other tests tomorrow." And that morning, before leaving: "Why don't you pray, instead of all this cross-examination of me?"

"What sort of prayer?" Krishna had asked naïvely.

"Well, you may say, 'O God, if You *are* there, save me if You can!' " the doctor replied, and guffawed loudly at his own joke. The doctor's humour was most trying.

Krishna realized that the doctor might sooner or later arrive at the correct diagnosis, but would it be within the patient's lifetime? He was appalled at the prospect of bereavement; his heart pounded wildly at the dreadful thought. Mars, having lain dormant, was astir now. Mars and an unidentified microbe had combined forces. The microbe was the doctor's business, however confused he might look. But the investigation of Mars was not.

Krishna hired a bicycle from a shop and pedalled off in the direction of the coconut grove where the old astrologer lived who had cast the horoscopes. He found the old man sitting in the hall, placidly watching a pack of children climb over walls, windows, furniture, and rice bags stacked in a corner and creating enough din to drown all conversation. He unrolled a mat for Krishna to sit on, and shouted over the noise of the children, "I told you at the start itself how it was going to turn out, but you people would not listen to my words. Yes, Mars has begun to exercise his most malignant aspect now. Under the circumstances, survival of the person concerned is doubtful." Krishna groaned. The children in a body had turned their attention to Krishna's bicycle, and were ringing the bell and feverishly attempting to push the machine off its stand. Nothing seemed to matter now. For a man about to lose his wife, the loss of a cycle taken on hire should not matter. Let children demolish all the bicycles in the town and Krishna would not care. Everything could be replaced except a human life.

"What shall I *do*?" he asked, picturing his wife in her bed asleep and never waking. He clung to this old man desperately, for he felt, in his fevered state of mind, that the astrologer could intercede with, influence, or even apologize on his behalf to, a planet in the high heavens. He remembered the reddish Mars he used to be shown in the sky when he was a Boy Scout—reddish on account of the malignity erupting like lava from its bosom. "What would you advise me to do? Please help me!" The old man looked over the rim of his spectacles at Krishna menacingly. His eyes were also red. Everything is red, reflected Krishna. He partakes of the tint of Mars. I don't know whether this man is my friend or foe. My doctor also has red eyes. So has the maid servant. . . . Red everywhere.

Krishna said, "I know that the ruling god in Mars is benign. I wish I knew how to propitiate him and gain his compassion."

The old man said, "Wait." He stood before a cupboard, took out a stack of palm-leaf strips with verses etched on them, four lines to a leaf. "This is one of the four originals of the *Brihad-Jataka,* from which the whole science of astrology is derived. This is what has given me my living;

when I speak, I speak with the authority of this leaf." The old man held the palm leaf to the light at the doorway and read out a Sanskrit aphorism: " 'There can be no such thing as evading fate, but you can insulate yourself to some extent from its rigours.' " Then he added, "Listen to this: 'Where Angaraka is malevolent, appease him with the following prayer . . . and accompany it with the gift of rice and gram and a piece of red silk. Pour the oblation of pure butter into a fire raised with sandal sticks, for four days continuously, and feed four Brahmins.' . . . Can you do it?"

Krishna was panic-stricken. How could he organize all this elaborate ritual (which was going to cost a great deal) when every moment and every rupee counted? Who would nurse his wife in his absence? Who would cook the ritual feast for the Brahmins? He simply would not be able to manage it unless his wife helped him. He laughed at the irony of it, and the astrologer said, "Why do you laugh at these things? You think you are completely modern?"

Krishna apologized for his laugh and explained his helpless state. The old man shut the manuscript indignantly, wrapped it in its cover, and put it away, muttering, "These simple steps you can't take to achieve a profound result. Go, go. . . . I can be of no use to you."

Krishna hesitated, took two rupees from his purse, and held them out to the old man, who waved the money away. "Let your wife get well first. Then give me the fee. Not now." And as Krishna turned to go: "The trouble is, your love is killing your wife. If you were an indifferent husband, she could survive. The malignity of Mars might make her suffer now and then, mentally more than physically, but would not kill her. I have seen horoscopes that were the exact replica of yours and the wife lived to a ripe age. You know why? The husband was disloyal or cruel, and that in some way neutralized the rigour of the planet in the Seventh House. I see your wife's time is getting to be really bad. Before anything happens, save her. If you can bring yourself to be unfaithful to her, try that. Every man with a concubine has a wife who lives long. . . ."

A strange philosophy, but it sounded feasible.

Krishna was ignorant of the technique of infidelity, and wished he had the slickness of his old friend Ramu, who in their younger days used to brag of his sexual exploits. It would be impossible to seek Ramu's guidance now, although he lived close by; he had become a senior government officer and a man of family and might not care to lend himself to reminiscences of this kind.

Krishna looked for a pimp representing the prostitutes in Golden Street and could not spot one, although the market gate was reputed to be swarming with them.

He glanced at his watch. Six o'clock. Mars would have to be appeased before midnight. Somehow his mind fixed the line at midnight. He turned homeward, leaned his bicycle on the lamppost, and ran up the steps of his house. At the sight of him the servant maid prepared to leave, but he begged her to stay on. Then he peeped into the sickroom, saw that his wife was asleep, and addressed her mentally, "You are going to get better soon. But it will cost something. Doesn't matter. Anything to save your life."

He washed hurriedly and put on a nylon shirt, a lace-edged dhoti, and a silk upper cloth; lightly applied some talcum and a strange perfume he had discovered in his wife's cupboard. He was ready for the evening. He had fifty rupees in his purse, and that should be adequate for the wildest evening one could want. For a moment, as he paused to take a final look at himself in the mirror, he was seized with an immense vision of passion and seduction.

He returned the hired cycle to the shop and at seven was walking up Golden Street. In his imagination he had expected glittering females to beckon him from their balconies. The old houses had pyols, pillars, and railings, and were painted in garish colours, as the houses of prostitutes were reputed to be in former times, but the signboards on the houses indicated that the occupants were lawyers, tradesmen, and teachers. The only relic of the old days was a little shop in an obscure corner that sold perfumes in coloured bottles and strings of jasmine flowers and roses.

Krishna passed up and down the street, staring hard at a few women here and there, but they were probably ordinary, indifferent housewives. No one returned his stare. No one seemed to notice his silk upper cloth and lace dhoti. He paused to consider whether he could rush into a house, seize someone, perform the necessary act, shed his fifty rupees, and rush out. Perhaps he might get beaten in the process. How on earth was one to find out which woman, among all those he had noticed on the terraces and verandahs of the houses, would respond to his appeal?

After walking up and down for two hours he realized that the thing was impossible. He sighed for the freedom between the sexes he read about in the European countries, where you had only to look about and announce your intentions and you could get enough women to confound the most malignant planet in the universe.

He suddenly remembered that the temple dancer lived somewhere here. He knew a lot of stories about Rangi of the temple, who danced before the god's image during the day and took lovers at night. He stopped for a banana and a fruit drink at a shop and asked the little boy serving him, "Which is the house of the temple dancer Rangi?" The boy was too small to understand the purport of his inquiry and merely replied, "I don't know." Krishna felt abashed and left.

Under a street lamp stood a jutka, the horse idly swishing its tail and the old driver waiting for a fare. Krishna asked, "Are you free?"

The driver sprang to attention. "Where do you wish to be taken, sir?"

Krishna said timidly, "I wonder if you know where the temple dancer Rangi lives?"

"Why do you want her?" the driver asked, looking him up and down.

Krishna mumbled some reply about his wanting to see her dance. "At this hour!" the driver exclaimed. "With so much silk and so much perfume on! Don't try to deceive me. When you come out of her house, she will have stripped you of all the silk and perfume. But tell me, first, why only Rangi? There are others, both experts and beginners. I will drive you wherever you like. I have carried hundreds like you on such an errand. But shouldn't I first take you to a milk shop where they will give you hot milk with crushed almond to give you stamina? Just as a routine, my boy. . . . I will take you wherever you want to go. Not my business anyway. Someone has given you more money than you need? Or is your wife pregnant and away at her mother's house? I have seen all the tricks that husbands play on their wives. I know the world, my master. Now get in. What difference does it make what you will look like when you come out of there? I will take you wherever you like."

Krishna obediently got into the carriage, filling its interior with perfume and the rustle of his silken robes. Then he said, "All right. Take me home."

He gave his address so mournfully that the jutka driver, urging his horse, said, "Don't be depressed, my young master. You are not missing anything. Someday you will think of this old fellow again."

"I have my reasons," Krishna began, gloomily.

The horse driver said, "I have heard it all before. Don't tell me." And he began a homily on conjugal life.

Krishna gave up all attempts to explain and leaned back, resigning himself to his fate.

Glossary

GLOSSARY

Angaraka: Mars
baksheesh: tip or gratuity
banian: under-vest
bhang: narcotic made from hemp
Brihad-Jataka: ancient work explaining the science of
    astrology
chokra: handy boy
Deepavali: festival of delights occurring in November
dhall: cooked and spiced lentils
dhobi: laundry boy or washerman
dhoti: sarong-like man's garment, tucked and knotted at
    the waist
jutka: two-wheeled carriage drawn by horse
Kali Yuga: the present era—last and darkest of the four
    ages of the world
kapi: coffee
lakh: a hundred thousand
Mahabharata: epic composed by Vyasa
mali: household gardener
moodhevi: goddess of adversity and all evil luck
paisa (plural *paise*): the smallest coin; one hundred paise

make a rupee, which is the equivalent of 7.5 cents
at the present rate of exchange

Parangi: foreigner (European)

Pongal: festival of harvest occurring in January

puja: worship, offering

pyol: platform for sitting, built along a house wall that faces
the street

Rama: the name of an avatar of Vishnu, and hero of
Ramayana

Ramayana: epic composed by Valmiki

sami: form of address similar to "sir"

Shiva: one of the three chief divinities (or trinity)

Sita: heroine of *Ramayana,* incarnation of Lakshmi, spouse
of god Vishnu

sloka: verse form in Sanskrit

swarga: heaven

Tamil: Dravidian language

veena: ancient stringed instrument

Yama Loka: the world of the god of death